PIECES
The Nu Romantics
"Redefining Romance"

A Collection by The Nu Romantics
...where light and dark come together in a beautiful mosaic.

Copyright © 2017 The Nu Romantics

PIECES of US

Copyright © 2017 The Nu Romantics
Cover Art by R.B. O'Brien
Interior Artwork by Wess. A. Haubrich
Formatting by Ashlee Shades
Kindle Edition
Published by: The Nu Romantics

The unauthorized reproduction or distribution of this copyrighted work is illegal. Criminal copyright infringement, including infringement without monetary gain, is investigated by the FBI and is punishable by up to 5 years in federal prison and a fine of $250,000.

Please purchase only authorized electronic editions, and do not participate in or encourage the electronic piracy of copyrighted materials. Your support of the author's rights is appreciated.

This book is a work of fiction. Names, characters, places, and incidents either are products of the author's imagination or are used fictitiously. Any resemblance to actual events or locales or persons, living or dead, is entirely coincidental.

THE NU ROMANTICS WAS FORMED TO REVOLT AGAINST THE PRECONCEIVED NOTIONS OF ROMANCE AND TO ELUCIDATE, THROUGH ALL MEDIUMS OF ART, PARTICULARLY WRITING, THAT THE "ROMANTIC" IS FOUND IN MORE THAN HAPPY ENDINGS, THAT IT CAN BE FOUND IN EVERYTHING FROM NATURE TO PAIN TO THE EROTIC TO EVEN DEATH...

The goal of The Nu Romantics is simple: To bring our mission to fruition and break stereotypes, which stems from the idea that "good" writing can be found in all genres and that to ignore the erotic as a separate category, unaccepted as some deviant endeavor, is foolish. With an emphasis on writing and technique and telling a story first, The Nu Romantics argue that romance and romantic are not synonyms. Romance is a genre that requires some semblance of a happy ending. Erotica focuses on titillation. The Nu Romantics are here to say that any writing that makes the reader feel, that uses language to create beauty, in nature or romance or even suffering and death, has its place. We are connected as humans in our life experiences, and if we can express that through art that renders emotion in a reader, including erotic aspects, that is romantic. A couple who takes their life is romantic. Saying goodbye to the one person you love is romantic. And watching a sunset when you know the world is about to end, that, too, is romantic.

Note from the authors:

This work is a collaboration of work from the authors featured within and consists of pieces of poetry and short stories from members of **The Nu Romantics**. And as fitting of our mission and goal, there are various themes found within this collection. Many pieces of work fit within more than one theme, so while you are reading this, you will see a poem or short story in more than one place. We wanted to guarantee each reader found the work best suited to their likes, and we didn't want to miss sharing each piece that would fit in that theme.

We hope you enjoy these "Pieces of Us," - where dark and light come together in a beautiful mosaic.

For more information about the Nu Romantics, please visit **thenuromantics.weebly.com**

Table of Contents

PIECES OF US — 2

HOPE AND NEW BEGINNINGS — 10

Two Lives Have Ended by Dab10 — 10

The Sound of His Voice by Denise Jury — 10

Solar Eclipse by R.B. O'Brien — 11

Take Me to The Edge by Debra Price — 12

Locked and Loaded by Kaye Donner — 13

Dreams by J. Molly B.C. — 13

For I Knew All Along You Were Mine by Xtina Marie — 15

SUPERNATURAL, UNEXPLAINED, AND HORROR — 17

Dark Demon by Ardent Rose — 17

Nothingness by Ashlee Shades — 18

The Spider's Lair by Bennet Lancaster — 21

What Blood Wants by Bryce Calderwood/Michael Martine — 22

Let Me In by R.B. O'Brien — 23

The Clan Gathers by Soliel De Bella — 25

Dreams by J. Molly B.C. — 25

ROMANTIC 27

Lover's Embrace by Ashlee Shades 27

The Sound of His Voice by Denise Jury 28

Kiss Me Forever by Seelie Kay 28

Revel in The Fire by Sebastian Nox 30

For I Knew All Along You Were Mine by Xtina Marie 30

I Want the Wild Lights by Sebastian Nox 32

I Enjoy Our Walks by Joe P Barrett 32

Long Distance Love by M.R. Wallace 34

Love Is Like the Ocean by Bennet Lancaster 35

Eternity's Bliss by Tori Dean and Bennet Lancaster 36

Locked and Loaded by Kaye Donner 36

Fall by Wess A. Haubrich 37

Hold My Hand by R.B. O'Brien 37

I Am Yours by Mystk Knight 38

EROTIC 39

Her Dream Lover by Ashlee Shades 39

Surrender by Tori Dean 44

My Soul Yearns by Melysza Jackson 45

What Blood Wants by Bryce Calderwood/Michael Martine 46

Take Me to The Edge by Debra Price 47

Dark Demon by Ardent Rose 48

Side Pocket: A Game of Billiards by Tori Dean	49
Darlin' by Debra Price	53
Joie de Vivre by Mystk Knight	54
Love-Making, Electric by R.B. O'Brien	64
His Pygmalion by Tamara McLanahan	67
Eternity's Bliss by Tori Dean and Bennet Lancaster	68
Revel in The Fire by Sebastian Nox	68
She Imagines by Carrie-Ann Hume	69
Submission by Melysza Jackson	70
The Ride by Athena Kelly	71
I Am Yours by Mystk Knight	71
The Sweetest Nectar by Tamara McLanahan	72

NOSTALGIA, LONGING, AND HEARTBREAK — 74

Kiss Me Forever by Seelie Kay	74
Long Distance Love by M.R. Wallace	76
My Soul Yearns by Melysza Jackson	76
No One by Dee See	77
Never Again by Claire Lawrence	78
I Want the Wild Lights by Sebastian Nox	79
Solar Eclipse by R.B. O'Brien	79
She Imagines by Carrie-Ann Hume	80
Fireworks, Fairies, and Men on the Moon by Karen Victoria Williams	81

Burn by Mystk Knight	82
Let Me In by R.B. O'Brien	83

ABOUT THE AUTHORS   85

R.B. O'BRIEN	85
ASHLEE SHADES	86
MYSTK KNIGHT	87
TORI DEAN	87
DEBRA PRICE	88
DENISE JURY	88
ARDENT ROSE	88
BENNET LANCASTER	89
SEELIE KAY	90
JOE P BARRETT	91
SOLIEL de BELLA	91
TAMARA MCLANAHAN	92
ATHENA KELLY	92
XTINA MARIE	93
DAB TEN	93
KAYE DONNER	94
WESS A. HAUBRICH	95
DEE SEE	95
J. MOLLY B.C.	96

CLAIRE LAWRENCE	**96**
KAREN WILLIAMS	**97**
M.R. WALLACE	**97**
CARRIE-ANN HUME	**98**
MELYSZA JACKSON	**98**
SEBASTIAN NOX	**99**
BRYCE CALDERWOOD	**99**

Hope and New Beginnings

Two Lives Have Ended by Dab10

Two lives have ended
One splash and I rowed away
New life is ahead

The Sound of His Voice by Denise Jury

The sound of his voice
A whisper of sweet nothings
Goosebumps aplenty

Music to my ears

Promises of things to come
Late night dalliance

Solar Eclipse by R.B. O'Brien

Like the moon
covering the sun,
Nature's humor
imparts an image,
painted surreal
onto the sky,
like our love,
where we weep
for its romanticism,
and marvel at the beauty
of darkness,
because we know Nature's
ephemeral prank,
that the light shall return
to its place
of centrality
in our world,
but not until the wind stills
and the birds hush
and our hearts listen to what
is lost,
and found,
in the sound of
our tears.
Distance is but
a beautiful solar eclipse,
the spaces between seconds
that let us know
the sincerity of yearning
in the blink of a hidden sun
behind an envious moon.

Take Me to The Edge by Debra Price

Take me to the edge of your reality
exploring the wilds of our hearts
Drink from the well of our existence

My journey of spirit, exploring the dark murky spaces
I came upon a place, in the midst of the nebulae
laying my head, I felt the soft moss-covered tree
closing eyes, I listened with senses
small messages, came sighing on scented wafts
whispering, to my wild core

Drink from my brook, fill yourself with my energy
where the secrets I glean

She came, laid her head upon my breast
her breath mingling, as she caressed
supping at my throat, kissing, nipping
nipples harden, now exposed
compelled, she calls me daemon
untamed vernal, wrapped in Time's embrace
we fill each other, angels grounded

Released from her embrace, I bow to her grace
thankfully deplete of regret, lost love
mine to find, again on journey's rest.

Locked and Loaded by Kaye Donner

Targets
acquired:
Locked
and Loaded.
Eyes held tightly across the room.
Neither chancing to blink.

Dreams by J. Molly B.C.

Every night
Another chance
I lie in bed
Reposed
A symphony of thoughts
Words fusing
My body still
My mind - sailing
My speculative perception
The sum of what is to be
One day
One night
The mystery
The anticipation
Eager
I allow myself to fall
Fall into a paradoxical sleep
The Magick
Veiled
The when
The how
His)O(alchemistical ways

They keep me restless by day
Hopeful by night
Within my Dreams
I land
Each time
Waiting to be found
Waiting
For the sound
The hand
The whisper

I wake
Resolute
Determined
To try again
Each night
I try
My endurance
Unwavering
I fall asleep
Floating pendulously
I SAIL
Through the Air
A TRAIN of prevailing Winds
Forevermore
Until I see
Until I hear
The whispered words I long to hear
It is TIME Sweetness
STAY

For I Knew All Along You Were Mine by Xtina Marie

(for my Sweetheart)

"How much do I love thee?"
Elizabeth said, "Let me count the ways"
But if I tried her method
I'm afraid we'd be here for days

Emily said, so eloquent,
"My river runs to thee"
But you are my river and my land
You're every leaf on every tree

I quote Paul as saying,
"Let us blend our souls as one"
But could he really know
Before you, there was none?

"Oh my Luve is like the melody,"
Robert said so very sweet
But did he know without you
My song was incomplete?

Anne said, "I prize thy love more
Than whole mines of gold"
And I understand this fully
For I will still love you when we are old

Ben told his precious Celia
"Time will not be ours forever"
But I am here to tell you that
My love will perish never

"But we loved with a love that was more than love"
Edgar wrote about Annabel Lee
And I feel in my soul he was writing about

Our hearts, that will never be free

Percy inquires
"Why not I with thine?"
And I have no choice but to agree
With his clever little rhyme

Christina wasn't the only one
"To say I loved you first"
But I'll say it better
Although not quite so well-rehearsed

Your eyes, they tell the truth
When all they do is shine
Dorthea said it best
"For I knew all along you were mine"

Supernatural, Unexplained, and Horror

Dark Demon by Ardent Rose

Deep in his soul the demon lies
His power appears in his eyes
Hypnotizing predator out for prey
With candles burning today is the day
His darkness bleeds through his touch
Consuming her in truculent lust
Chains restrain her to his will
Caution the danger is his thrill
Sweat drips and her breaths hitch
Falling tighter in his grip
Her glowing skin takes the whip
His strength never tires

Soon her screams will expire
Body and mind soaring higher
The demon rests, finally sated
Allows the man within elated
Solace returns only for a time
The beast in his darkness will revive...

Nothingness by Ashlee Shades

The cemetery ground was blanketed in a thick cloud of fog as they crept closer to the edge of the cliff overlooking the sea and waves below. The darkness of the night lent an eerie sensation to the evening, which was all the better; it would make this evening even more memorable. She loved taking the men to the cliff before she put them down.
"I can't believe tonight is the night," Charles spoke in a hushed voice. She knew he was excited for the night. She had kept him waiting to consummate their RELATIONSHIP for well over a month. She kept them all waiting because as soon as they had a taste of her, they would say goodbye to this world.
None of them knew it. None of them had even the slightest idea they would be meeting their end after she sent them to impossible heights of ecstasy. She was a beautiful woman, with curves in all the right places, and she knew how to make them work to her advantage. Women wanted to be her, and men just wanted her.
They wanted her lips on them.
They wanted her hands roaming their body.
They wanted to bury themselves deep within her sex, settle between her thighs.
She loved it. She fed off their excitement, loved leading them on until just the right moment.
"Not much longer, it's just past that tree standing over there."
It was HER tree. It was the place she led each of them for the rendezvous. It was where she granted them their wish to taste her, to sample her sweet nectar.

"Hurry," he whispered. She laughed to herself. He had no fucking idea that he was only rushing his own demise. Such a boy. Such a little, fucking boy.

She picked up her pace until they finally made it to the spot. She stopped and told him to undress.

She took off her dress and hung it on the lowest tree branch hanging near her head. She loved it and didn't want anything to happen to it. It would be such a shame if it did, she had splurged when she purchased it last week. She wanted something special for this occasion.

She bought something new for each one. Her closet was filled with memorabilia commemorating each time. Over a dozen in all, and each one more beautiful than the last.

She sauntered over to the spot he was standing, staring at her in awe. They all did that. She loved the attention, but these looks were all the same by now.

She knelt before him on the damp ground and grasped his throbbing cock. She looked up at him and kept her eyes glued to him...eye contact was important for them to feel a connection with her. She wasn't completely heartless after all.

She opened her mouth and wrapped her beautiful, full, red lips around his tip. Just a little tease for now.

Her tongue flicked over the small hole at the tip, licking the moisture beading there. The musky flavor was all male, and one of her favorite tastes. She loved doing this: sucking cock. She loved the control it gave her over the men. Her arousal intensified, her sex dampened with her slickness, her clit began to throb in need.

Her free hand wandered between her legs and circled her engorged nub. She rode her hand as her mouth worked on his member. When her orgasm hit her, she moaned around his cock. The humming vibration caused him to grow even fuller in her mouth, and right before he came, she pulled away.

"Lay down. I'm going to ride you as you've never been ridden before. You are going to be fucked...to DEATH."

He had no idea that she meant those words literally. None of them ever knew, never had a clue until they were falling, or bleeding, or struggling to catch their breath.

When he was on his back, she straddled him and slid his cock into her wetness. Ahh...this felt so damn good. The fullness of him inside her, hitting that sweet spot deep within – it was HEAVEN.

With each bounce on his cock, her full breasts jiggled. She covered them with her hands and played with her erect nipples. The pinching and tugging sent tingles and thrills throughout her body. The only thing that could surpass this feeling, the feeling she got after an orgasm, was when she had control over the life or death of the man she had chosen. Seeing or watching the life leave them, knowing she was the last person they would see when they met their eternity – that was the most arousing and erotic feeling in the world.

She began riding him faster and harder, sliding up and then dropping down, grinding her clit into his pelvic area. She added a few circular motions for additional pleasure. Why not give him a few more moments of joy before he came to an end?

And come he would when she was ready.

She came down one final time before an explosive climax took over. She screamed out his name over and over as her cum covered his cock, which was ready to fill her.

She looked down into his eyes and told him, "Come for me now. Fill me."

Like a good little bitch, he did. He thrust up into her and spilled his release into her waiting core. Spurt after spurt of his cum filled her until it was oozing out of her and covering him. She dipped her fingers into the liquid and sucked the juices from her fingers.

"Damn, that's so fucking hot," he commented at the sight.

"Come, I have something I need to show you just over there," she pointed to the ledge.

Standing, she offered her hand to help him to his feet and led him to the spot she wanted to assert control one more time.

She pointed to the horizon, where the lighthouse was shining its light, a beacon for ships at sea.

"You see that?" She asked him.

"The lighthouse?" He questioned, confused and curious.

"Yeah, the lighthouse. You need to let it guide you."

"What is that supposed to mean?"

"You'll find out." She stepped closer to the edge, and like a good little boy, he followed.

"It's a long drop," she told him.

"Yes, it is."

She looked up at him and said, "I'm sorry."

"For what?" He asked her.

"For this."

And with a slight shove, he was soaring, then falling into the crashing waves below.
She smirked, her job well done, and sang the closing lines to her favorite song:
"Yesterday seems as though it never existed
Death greets me warm, now I will just say goodbye
Goodbye…"

The Spider's Lair by Bennet Lancaster

He beckons out
to those
who have lost their way.
Poetic words spoken
to lure them in.
Promises
of freedom
fantasies
lust
and more.
His web has been woven
with the utmost care.
Beautiful
Enticing
shimmering in the sun.
Ensnared you will be
if to his words
you give heed.
Proceed with caution
act with care
or one more prize
will be added
to the spider's lair.

What Blood Wants by Bryce Calderwood/Michael Martine

What does blood want?
That was the question. Every night Ashlyn Kovalenko asked it, like a prayer, before setting out to hunt.
She raised her glass and signaled to the futa club's bartender, a lithe young futa named Judith, who came over looking apprehensive. It looked good on her.
"I don't know if I should give you more," she said, gently rubbing her forearm, which was covered by a turned sleeve cuff. Ashlyn smiled, revealing her fangs.
"I'll pay double the usual."
Judith scowled. "It's not the money. I could've kicked you out months ago. Every few weeks you're back, though, and I get excited every time I see you come in the door."
The woman looked at her with a pleading hint in her eyes but dropped her gaze. She busied herself removing Ashlyn's martini glass, the interior of which was filmed in red.
"You want to know why?"
She nodded.
"Let me have my drink and I'll tell you."
She fetched top shelf vodka and splashed some into a martini glass. She set down a shot glass and dashed some into it, as well. After looking around to see if anyone watched amid the chaos of the club, she pushed up her sleeve.
On Ashlyn's ring finger was an ornate, gold claw sporting a carved skull cameo against a black background. A gold chain connected it to a ring further back on her finger to hold it on. Her other fingers sported long, pointed, black-lacquered nails. She flipped up the cameo on its hinge, revealing a tiny slider switch. Using the nail on her other hand she pushed the slider, extending a thick but sharp stainless-steel needle.
She dipped the needle into the shot glass of vodka, held Judith's wrist with one hand, and grasped her elbow with the hand sporting the claw. Judith tensed and sucked in a breath through her teeth as the needle punctured her skin. Blood trickled off her elbow and into the glass. It clouded within the vodka at first, but within seconds there was more blood than vodka in the glass.

"Now tell me," said Judith, pressing tissues to her arm.
Ashlyn raised the glass to her lips and breathed in its aroma, closing her eyes for a second. She took a sip, enjoying the small amount of alcohol her body could accept.
"The answer is as obvious as it is unbelievable," Ashlyn said.
At first, Judith scowled again, more severely, but then her face slackened into resigned sadness.
"Why do I always fall for the crazy ones?" Judith lamented.
"All right, then," said Ashlyn, "You tell me. Why blood? What does blood want?"
"Love," said Judith. "It wants love."
Ashlyn flinched. With a trembling hand she set her drink down. Of course. It was so simple, wasn't it?
"You're such a beautiful soul. Will you love me, tonight?" she asked.
"I thought you'd never ask," said Judith.
Ashlyn hated herself for what she was about to do.

Let Me In by R.B. O'Brien

"Let me in."
I rolled over, the familiar voice, a figment of my waking dreams, the rain banging against my window, making me hallucinate, hear things. I hated the rain, its insistent hammer. It seemed to always rain here in the mountains. I swear it rained every time I missed him, which seemed to be always.
"Wake up."
I heard it again, and yet didn't. My arms pimpled with goosebumps, and I sat up in bed, uneasy, a cold sweat lacing my body. I turned on a light and rubbed my weary eyes. The curtain on my window, moved, billowy, as if a figure circled it. I was certain I had closed the window tight, but the wind must still have been coming through the cracks. I drew my legs against my chest and hugged them, trying to soothe myself from the tremors rising, uncontrollable.
Riley stood up next to me on the bed, having been roused from slumber himself. Wagging his tail, his floppy white ears peaked and brown eyes

pleading, his insistence made me laugh a little, and it subdued the rising panic I felt.

"Oh. So, it's you who's waking me." I smiled and gave my Bichon Frise a little pat, a gift my husband had given me when he proposed, even though he was allergic to dogs. "Not now, Riley." I pointed at the window. "You'll soak us both."

The rain slammed louder against the window, and I stood, drawn to the curtain and its movement, like a dance, mesmerizing me. Riley began to growl, and my unease grew. I tensed, and yet I walked, trance-like, to the window. Something told me not to open the curtain, a voice deep within me, but my feet began its march, one foot in front of the other, methodic, metal drawn to magnet.

Slowly, I reached out to the curtain. My blood whooshed inside my eardrums, Riley's growl intensifying. Goosebumps turned to chills. I placed one hand on the curtain and gripped my flimsy nightgown tight around my neck with the other to try to ease the draft that seemed to push the curtains' dance onward faster, but fear was palpable. Like a rubbernecker drawn to the scene of an accident, I couldn't stop myself from moving the drapery aside to look out the window. *Just open the curtain*, I told myself. *See that it's just the rain.*

Like pulling off an adhesive band-aid, I ripped open the curtain, my instincts highly attuned, my nerves strung like guitar strings ready to snap. *No!* I screamed, a death cry, a howl that echoed against the panes. I recognized with clarity the woman through the fog and mist. *No!* I said again, whimpering, and my body crumpled to the floor with more wails. *It can't be!*

I craned my neck over my right shoulder to look back towards my bed from the window, and what I saw stopped me from breathing, the scene, a tableau from my past. I thought I had moved on from it, but it haunted me relentlessly, like the rain against the window.

Lying dead, I saw my husband sprawled out the way I remembered him dying in his sleep that fateful night all those years ago. I turned my eyes once again to the window, gripping my nightgown tighter still to fight the cold that took residence in every fiber of my being. Fright. Confusion. A silent scream as I stood motionless, mouth agape.

The woman staring at me through the window was me, her eyes, round coals, as black as the night sky. My corporeal body lay dead, too, next to him on top of the white wedding sheets, covered in red.

The Clan Gathers by Soliel De Bella

The clan gathers in the darkness,
peace unveils chaos.
Under this night's moon,
they will seek the flesh of those souls they need for their own delight.
Trust naught the stranger whom attempts your acquaintance,
as he is certainly your foe.

Dreams by J. Molly B.C.

Every night
Another chance
I lie in bed
Reposed
A symphony of thoughts
Words fusing
My body still
My mind - sailing
My speculative perception
The sum of what is to be
One day
One night
The mystery
The anticipation
Eager
I allow myself to fall
Fall into a paradoxical sleep

The Magick
Veiled
The when
The how
His)O(alchemistical ways
They keep me restless by day
Hopeful by night
Within my Dreams
I land
Each time
Waiting to be found
Waiting
For the sound
The hand
The whisper

I wake
Resolute
Determined
To try again
Each night
I try
My endurance
Unwavering
I fall asleep
Floating pendulously
I SAIL
Through the Air
A TRAIN of prevailing Winds
Forevermore
Until I see
Until I hear
The whispered words I long to hear
It is TIME Sweetness
STAY

Romantic

Lover's Embrace by Ashlee Shades

He stares at me with a gleam in his eyes,
I know then what's in store.
His firm hands roam up my thighs,
I moan and beg for more.

His breath dances across my skin,
leaving a heated trail in its wake.
To feel this way is surely a sin,
the punishment of which I'll gladly take.

His hands glide across my back,

his lips caressing my spine.
His fingers sweep the hair from my neck,
his touch says, "You are mine."

His arms wrap around me,
holding me in place.
I'm in my favorite place to be,
I'm safe in my lover's embrace.

The Sound of His Voice by Denise Jury

The sound of his voice
A whisper of sweet nothings
Goosebumps aplenty

Music to my ears
Promises of things to come
Late night dalliance

Kiss Me Forever by Seelie Kay

I stare outside the hospital window and take in the bleak sky. How appropriate for what is to come. I turn and look lovingly at the man who lies before me, his thin body no longer hooked up to tubes or machines. His breath is shallow. His time, limited.
This man is my husband of more than sixty years. Together we have raised six children, grand-partnered fifteen, and great grand-partnered thirty more. We have lived a good life, one filled with struggles, but also much love. And now that life is about to end, as one of us is called to the great beyond.
I am lost. I am afraid. I do not know if I can go on.

He is not only my husband you see, but my lover and Master of many years. We were kinky before kinky was cool. We had a 50s household before it became something to which younger generations aspired. This man was my adored Dominant, and I, his cherished submissive. We played, we laughed, we trusted, we loved.

While we raised our children, my Master traveled often for his job. Whenever we were to be apart for more than a day, he would pull me into his strong embrace, and whisper, "Kiss me forever." And I did. I put so much passion and so much love into each kiss that he often claimed I curled his toes. Our children claimed they could see smoke coming out of his ears.

But those kisses meant a lot to us. We understood that life was fickle, that it could end at any moment. We knew that there was always a chance that he would not return. So, I had to make sure that if that kiss was to be our last, it was a good one.

I have thought of those kisses often over the past few days, as my Master drifts in and out of consciousness. His moments of wakening have been brief. He has not spoken a single word. Fearful that if he did awaken, he would find me crying, I have held back my tears. Those can be shed another day. They will not heal, nor will they make my Master's suffering any less.

A nurse comes in to check on my Master. She walks over to me, puts a hand on my arm and says kindly,

"It won't be long now."

I nod, fighting those tears that want to flow, and walk over to the bed. I pull back the covers and lie down beside this man I love. I rest my head on his chest. His heart is weak. It seems to be beating sporadically, as if each beat is a struggle, a losing battle. I drift off.

Suddenly, I awake. My Master seems to be struggling. I sit up and gaze into his now-open blue eyes. He seems confused. I take his hand and whisper, "Master?"

He smiles slightly then, and says softly, "Kiss me forever."

I lean down and kiss him with the same passion I possessed in my 20s. My kiss is hard and thorough. Every ounce of love I feel for this man is in that kiss. If it is to be our last, I want him to know that I love him to the depth of my soul. I want his last thought to be of that kiss.

When I break the kiss, he again smiles. "Good girl," he says. Moments later, he takes his last breath.

And finally, I cry.

Revel in The Fire by Sebastian Nox

Revel in the fire
of the old gods
piety is absent
from their gaze
blood is not supped
from chalice ornate
it trickles
from hungry
lips
marked by ivory
passion
tongue
the vessel
swirl copper
truth
in mouths
where carnal hymns
recited
in breathy exhalations

For I Knew All Along You Were Mine by Xtina Marie

(for my Sweetheart)

"How much do I love thee?"
Elizabeth said, "Let me count the ways"
But if I tried her method
I'm afraid we'd be here for days

Emily said, so eloquent,
"My river runs to thee"
But you are my river and my land
You're every leaf on every tree

I quote Paul as saying,
"Let us blend our souls as one"
But could he really know
Before you, there was none?

"Oh my Luve is like the melody,"
Robert said so very sweet
But did he know without you
My song was incomplete?

Anne said, "I prize thy love more
Than whole mines of gold"
And I understand this fully
For I will still love you when we are old

Ben told his precious Celia
"Time will not be ours forever"
But I am here to tell you that
My love will perish never

"But we loved with a love that was more than love"
Edgar wrote about Annabel Lee
And I feel in my soul he was writing about
Our hearts, that will never be free

Percy inquires
"Why not I with thine?"
And I have no choice but to agree
With his clever little rhyme

Christina wasn't the only one
"To say I loved you first"
But I'll say it better
Although not quite so well-rehearsed

Your eyes, they tell the truth
When all they do is shine
Dorthea said it best
"For I knew all along you were mine"

I Want the Wild Lights by Sebastian Nox

I want the wild lights
of your eyes
fire in a stone circle
beacon to an indifferent sea
windswept flame
burning salt of
my tears
in the hungry tongue
of your gaze

I Enjoy Our Walks by Joe P Barrett

Leaving footprints in the sand on a sunny summer day
holding hands, talking, laughing, giving kisses, and hugs.
We sit on the beach holding each other 'til the sun fades into the ocean.

I stand and offer my hand to you and ask for a dance.

Crunchy footsteps on a beautiful crisp autumn day
holding hands, talking, laughing, giving kisses, and hugs.
We pull each other to the ground and wrestle
trying to tickle each other in the fallen leaves and settle down for a picnic.
We read to each other 'til the sun disappears behind the trees.

I stand offer my hand to you and ask for a dance.

Fresh footprints in a new fallen snow
holding hands, talking, laughing, giving kisses, and hugs.
A snow ball fight giggles and warm kisses,
we talk as we build a snow man and a snow woman side by side.
We sit on a blanket talk and hold each other to keep warm 'til the snow is
        flickering in the street lights.

I stand offer my hand to you and ask for a dance.

Walking on fresh grown grass on a spring day
holding hands, talking, laughing, giving kisses, and hugs
grabbing each other, rolling in the grass, tickling, kissing, and laughing.
We talk as we plant flowers.
We rub and throw dirt on each other 'til the sun turns to a soft spring rain.

I stand offer my hand to you and ask for a dance.

I love our walks.

Long Distance Love by M.R. Wallace

It was like a mountain, honestly. Though he would've preferred scaling a physical peak to get to her. Any day. The months stretched out before him in slow agony.
Long distance relationships were always difficult. He knew that. He'd had them before. Though, looking back now, it was hard to call those bouts of juvenile affection anything more than what they were: The inexpert fumblings of teenage attraction mixed with socially awkward habits. But this, this was decidedly more.
It was real. It was raw. They'd come a long way from their first digital 'Hi there'.
It was supposed to be some lighthearted fun, he mused. Just a chance to get to explore themselves, who they really were underneath. They had been stupid to think they could undertake such a task without deeper repercussions. Love had struck, hard and fast, and left them both breathless.
He spun his phone in his fingers, like he used to do with CDs. His lips pursed. This was the second worst part.
The waiting.
It was always there at the forefront, hopelessly entwined with the time remaining until they could be together. He fretted and worried, moving his lower jaw right and left, another holdover from his youth.
Buzz. Ding.
He hit the lock button, the screen illuminating in his hands. Her name sat atop the pile of other notifications, all the ones he could do without as long as she was still there.
"Hey, baby."
His heart fluttered, his pulse beginning to quicken. For just another moment, he was on top of the world again.

Love Is Like the Ocean by Bennet Lancaster

Love is like the ocean.
Thrilling when first entered
captivating to say the least.
Your every thought is consumed
by what lies before thee.
At times it is so hot
it is almost too much to bear.
Others times
it is deathly cold.
Yet it is still the same.
Smooth as glass one moment.
The next a storm has brewed
punishing everything in its path
only because it is there.
The storm is not the ocean.
The storm merely affects it.
Love is affected the same way
by the storms of life.
The ocean is vast
seemingly endless
waiting to be explored.
Such is love.
To truly discover
what is being offered
one has to leave the shore
venture out
dive into its depths
to truly experience
all the wonders
which lie in store.

Eternity's Bliss by Tori Dean and Bennet Lancaster

As the sun goes down
Passions rise
The need to once more
Feel alive

A caress
Followed by a kiss
Show me, my Dear
What I have missed

Breathless moans
Embers ignited
Burning deep
She pleases me

Stopping mid-caress
She looks at me
Let me show you
How much you're missed

My pleasure is your pleasure
My love is your love
Let's join as one
And fall into eternity's bliss

Locked and Loaded by Kaye Donner

Targets
acquired:
Locked

and Loaded.
Eyes held tightly across the room.
Neither chancing to blink.

Fall by Wess A. Haubrich

Fall
into me
on our island
of serenity
Let me
hold you
until
the seasons
stop changing

Hold My Hand by R.B. O'Brien

Hold my hand
as we enter
the old bookstore
where our smiles
meet secrets
of Collins
and Hall
and Mr. Shakespeare,
and our souls filter,
like one ray of sunlight
in a room full of floating dust,
the pages of us

reflected in living prose.
Sigh the verses
through the very fingertips
that traced love's
nightly visits
over bare bodies
and whispered through wet eyes,
"I love you,"
in eternal etched kisses.

I Am Yours by Mystk Knight

Bind me by your trust
Hold me with your actions
Secure me by understanding
Enrapture me with your touch

The day is yours to seize
But the night, ahh the night
Must be won with drops
of pleasure and
Splashes of excruciating joy

Rain down on my flesh
Soak me with your essence
Leave me breathless
in anticipation
Make me beg to be tipped
into the rushing fall

I am yours

Erotic

Her Dream Lover by Ashlee Shades

He came to her again; stalked toward her in all his naked male glory. He was gorgeous, and she loved staring at him as he walked toward her bed. He knelt beside her, and his eyes roamed the length of her body, from toes to her breasts and back down again. His gaze left a heated trail in its wake, and a yearning from deep within her for more from him. More of his touch.
And then it happened.
His hand slowly crept up her firm, naked thigh, moved across her hip and to the hollow of her abdomen where it rested while his lips kissed their way over the mounds of her swollen breasts. The passion stirring deep within her was overwhelming, almost too much to handle. He knew just where to touch her, where to kiss, where to lick. He played her body like an instrument that was designed specifically for him. She writhed beneath him, sliding her hands up and down the taut muscles of his back. She dug

her nails into the sweaty flesh and relished in the hiss of his breath as her nails sunk into the skin.

"Keep that up, Sweetheart, and you may end up with a punishment instead," he warned her. His voice: deep and velvety, and smooth like melted chocolate only made her desire for him intensify.

"You're already punishing me. You know you are," she groaned when her lover laughed at her. This torturous foreplay of his was sending her senses on a yo-yo obstacle course. He took her to unimaginable heights, right to that edge, and then he slowly brought her back down again. Over, and over he had been doing this, and her body was hypersensitive now.

How long had they been at this game? An hour? Two? She honestly didn't know. The pleasure his expert touch ignited robbed her of all thought – of all awareness of everything except for him. Her entire world at this very moment centered on this man in her arms, in her bed, in her body.

She couldn't even remember the day, month, year. Everything was forgotten, and the only thing in her mind was this: painful, torturous pleasure he was putting her through. It was always like this with him.

His body moved up hers even more now, the coarse hair covering his muscular legs chaffed her smooth skin and sent butterflies of excitement fluttering throughout her body, causing a tingling down to her toes. His rough, calloused hands glided back up her stomach, across her ribs, and cupped one of her firm breasts. He bent his head to take one pert nipple into his warm, wet mouth and he sucked, nipped, and soothed with a flick of his tongue. The swirling around the tip of her nipple was sending tiny bursts of shocking sensations to her stomach and then further on, increasing the arousal that was waiting to grant his hardness the entrance she prayed he would be seeking soon.

"Please," she begged him when his mouth covered her other breast, his hand squeezing it.

"Not yet, Princess. I am not about to rush through this."

Her hips began undulating as his tongue teased her erect nipple again, his hand moving to her free breast to play, or torture her. Her breathing grew more labored as she struggled for air amidst the overpowering arousal her body was experiencing.

After what felt like months, years, but was mere seconds, a few minutes, tops, his mouth was working its way up the column of her throat, his tongue darting out to lick at the pulse beating at the base of her neck. Then, he moved to her ear, whispering sweet nothings in a low, breathy voice that caused her arousal to shoot to new heights. He spoke promises to her of what he was going to do to her, to her body, in minute detail that left no doubt in her mind that she would be left completely sated, pleasured beyond belief – more so than ever before. Completely wrecked, but without remorse or regret.

His hand roamed down her body once again, stopping at that sweet spot between her legs where the moisture from her sex heated and dampened her upper thighs, lubricating her lower body in anticipation of his intrusion. The swollen nub was tender, and she almost jumped off the bed the moment his finger made contact with the sensitive flesh. He tapped it, lightly, and she almost screamed from the painful pleasure it was sending throughout her body. Then his taps turned harder, the contact with her clit firmer until finally, his finger stayed there rubbing circles. It hurt so bad. So. Damn. Bad.

"I can't... take any more," she moaned. Her back arched and her hips lifted.

"Yes, you can," his voice came to her, commanding her obedience. "You will."

And like a good little girl, her hips lowered to the bed, but wouldn't still. The pressure was building inside her, screaming and clawing for a release. A release which had long been denied her body by his expert touch. She was burning. She was on fire, and his touch, his attention, was the only thing that could calm the flame it had ignited.

"Please," she begged.

"Not yet, Sweetheart," his words washed over her, engulfing her in HIM. How was she supposed to live after this? This had been going on for far too long.

He moved his head down her body, his tongue sliding through the valley between her breasts to the dip of her stomach, and lower still, to the place where his hand was waiting. She looked down at him, and he raised his eyes to meet her gaze before his head dipped down and his tongue darted out again. One lick on the tip of her sensitive clit caused her breath to catch in her already dry throat. That lick was followed by another lick, then another, and finally, his lips covered her nub and kissed it.

It was one of the most erotic things she had ever felt. This game, his touch, his kiss, this painful yet pleasurable torture was more than she had ever experienced before, and it was overwhelming. She couldn't breathe. She couldn't speak or think.

Her eyes rolled back, and her head sunk further into her pillows. She inhaled, deeply, and her chest rose in the air, her firm breasts pointing toward the ceiling. His mouth continued its ministrations, and he tenderly kissed and sucked at her clit as his fingers played at the opening of her sex.

He closed his mouth over her and hummed. She could feel the vibrations in her core.

When he took her clit into his mouth again, he sucked even harder than before and his fingers, now coated with her slick juices, entered her sex. One finger, followed by a second, and then a third. Her toes curled down as she clenched his fingers and sucked them deep within her welcoming heat.

"God!" She couldn't contain the plea.

"Not God, Sweetheart. Me. Remember who it is who is bringing you this pleasure." His voice was even deeper, huskier than before. "Look at me," he commanded.

She couldn't open her eyes. She was in heaven and hell, both. Heaven because of the sheer ecstasy and hell because of the torture. She shook her head 'no.'

When she didn't do as he commanded, he removed his mouth from her clit and smacked it. The slap shocked her, and she gasped.

"I said look at me, Sweetheart."

This time she did. Slowly, she opened her eyes and lifted her head enough to see him.

"When you call out a name it will be mine and no one else's. I am the one who controls your pleasure, your pain. Your body is mine to command. Do you hear me? I am its Master."

She couldn't speak. He had never been this... this... dominating before, and she didn't know how to take it, so she just nodded her head.

"I promise you; you will feel nothing but passion with me. Always. It pleasures me to see you writhing beneath my hands. It arouses me to see the ecstasy grace your beautiful face, to see your perfect body flushed with pleasure that my touch brings."

If she hadn't been close to coming before, she was now. Those words hit her in a place she didn't want to think about.

She nodded again, and he resumed lavishing attention on her body. This time though, he thrust his fingers harder, deeper inside her and they were hitting, rubbing, and pressing on that sweet spot that always drove her crazy. His touch became more determined, more precise. He was proving a point to her: he owned her.

With as much as he was putting her body through she was taking it. Her body opened for him. It craved him more than anything or anyone ever before. She dug her fingers into the sheets again, bunching them up within her fists and holding tight.

She moaned. She couldn't help it or hold it back any longer. Her orgasm was boiling, and she was ready to burst from the pressure.

He lifted his head and said, "I can feel your walls trying to push me out, Sweetheart. Your body is ready. Come for me. Now."

As soon as his mouth was back on her, she let go and screamed his name as her body released all it had been holding back. He stayed there lapping at her entrance, drinking up the juices that flowed from her opening.

When her climax had abated, and she was able to breathe again, he withdrew his fingers and lifted them to her mouth.

"Taste yourself, Sweetheart."

She opened her mouth and allowed him to insert his fingers. She could taste the tangy, sweet essence of HER. She sucked his fingers clean from her cum, maintaining eye contact with him as she did.

He withdrew his fingers and covered her mouth with his, capturing her lips in a punishing kiss that stole her breath all over again. His tongue licked at the seam of her mouth, and she parted her lips to grant him access, again.

He reached the side table to retrieve protection and made quick work of covering himself before moving between her legs. She wrapped her thighs around his and tugged the back of his head to bring his mouth even closer, pulling his body tighter to hers.

She couldn't get him close enough. But she held him there, sealing their lips together as he readied himself.

He took himself in his hands and guided his cock to her entrance and pressed into her folds. Her slickness allowed him to move in smoothly and inch by inch he glided in until her full fully blanketed within her channel.

He broke the kiss to move his lips to her neck, whispering along the way, "You feel... so... damn good."

"Ooohhh," she moaned, loving the feel of his lips and breath on the nape of her neck.

He lifted his ass in the air, pulling out of her until only the tip of him was still in, and then he surged forward, slamming his tip against the deepest walls of her sex.

"Fuck," she screamed. It was too much.

It wasn't enough.

Again, he pulled back and slammed in. This was no lovemaking session this time. No. This was a primal mating, a sating of dark, carnal desires. Her need and hunger matched his and took over.

She met him thrust for thrust, their bodies leaving no space between them as they moved against one another. Sweat-slickened bodies glided against one another.

The scent of sex mixed with sweat permeated the air and drove her crazy as she ran her nails up the tautness of his back. He grunted, from the exertion from their sex or the pain of her nails in his flesh, she didn't know, nor did she care. All she cared about at that moment was reaching that peak again, with him.
One of his hands moved to her head, and he grabbed a fistful of her hair, tugging it slightly. The pain barely felt as it was overpowered by the pleasure of his member sliding out and slamming into her. He moved his other hand to her thigh and squeezed as he held it against his hip.
She couldn't hold back any longer. She needed to let go.
"I'm going... to... come," she gasped. Her walls tightened around him and began to contract.
He lifted his head back and roared, "Fuuuck!"
She felt his cock throbbing inside of her as he came. The pulsing prolonging her climax as it worked against the contracting of her walls. Finally, when their orgasms subsided, and their panting and breathing calmed, and their racing hearts returned to a normal pace, he lifted himself from her body.
And just like every time before, she reached out for him as he walked away.
She called out his name as he disappeared, dissolving into nothing.

Isabelle woke up coated in sweat, her throat dry and sore from her heavy, rapid breathing.
She had the dream again.
Maybe one day she would meet him...

Surrender by Tori Dean

In that soft sexy velvety voice
that ignites my inner core
Heat rising between my legs
Making me clench
Throb
I need you inside me

Consuming
Taming the raging fire within
Make love to me
As I surrender to you
Mind
Body
Soul
I am yours
Show me
Pleasure me
Play me
Make me sing
My desires are your desires
I want you
Need you
I am yours

My Soul Yearns by Melysza Jackson

My soul yearns for a soothing touch
I stand waiting for this so much
My thoughts churn like a tornado's demand
My soul screams its taught command
Rain does not yield to such ultimatum
When I shrink down to my knees before him
Letting go my turbulent thoughts
Tears follow a heavy onslaught
A soothing caress pebbles my flesh
Sweet moan escapes, a single breath
As my soul connects to the soothing rain's touch

What Blood Wants by Bryce Calderwood/Michael Martine

What does blood want?
That was the question. Every night Ashlyn Kovalenko asked it, like a prayer, before setting out to hunt.
She raised her glass and signaled to the futa club's bartender, a lithe young futa named Judith, who came over looking apprehensive. It looked good on her.
"I don't know if I should give you more," she said, gently rubbing her forearm, which was covered by a turned sleeve cuff. Ashlyn smiled, revealing her fangs.
"I'll pay double the usual."
Judith scowled. "It's not the money. I could've kicked you out months ago. Every few weeks you're back, though, and I get excited every time I see you come in the door."
The woman looked at her with a pleading hint in her eyes but dropped her gaze. She busied herself removing Ashlyn's martini glass, the interior of which was filmed in red.
"You want to know why?"
She nodded.
"Let me have my drink and I'll tell you."
She fetched top shelf vodka and splashed some into a martini glass. She set down a shot glass and dashed some into it, as well. After looking around to see if anyone watched amid the chaos of the club, she pushed up her sleeve.
On Ashlyn's ring finger was an ornate, gold claw sporting a carved skull cameo against a black background. A gold chain connected it to a ring further back on her finger to hold it on. Her other fingers sported long, pointed, black-lacquered nails. She flipped up the cameo on its hinge, revealing a tiny slider switch. Using the nail on her other hand, she pushed the slider, extending a thick but sharp stainless-steel needle.
She dipped the needle into the shot glass of vodka, held Judith's wrist with one hand, and grasped her elbow with the hand sporting the claw. Judith tensed and sucked in a breath through her teeth as the needle punctured her skin. Blood trickled off her elbow and into the glass. It clouded within the vodka at first, but within seconds there was more blood than vodka in the glass.

"Now tell me," said Judith, pressing tissues to her arm.
Ashlyn raised the glass to her lips and breathed in its aroma, closing her eyes for a second. She took a sip, enjoying the small amount of alcohol her body could accept.
"The answer is as obvious as it is unbelievable," Ashlyn said.
At first, Judith scowled again, more severely, but then her face slackened into resigned sadness.
"Why do I always fall for the crazy ones?" Judith lamented.
"All right, then," said Ashlyn, "You tell me. Why blood? What does blood want?"
"Love," said Judith. "It wants love."
Ashlyn flinched. With a trembling hand she set her drink down. Of course. It was so simple, wasn't it?
"You're such a beautiful soul. Will you love me, tonight?" she asked.
"I thought you'd never ask," said Judith.
Ashlyn hated herself for what she was about to do.

Take Me to The Edge by Debra Price

Take me to the edge of your reality
exploring the wilds of our hearts
Drink from the well of our existence

My journey of spirit, exploring the dark murky spaces
I came upon a place, in the midst of the nebulae
laying my head, I felt the soft moss-covered tree
closing eyes, I listened with senses
small messages, came sighing on scented wafts
whispering, to my wild core

Drink from my brook, fill yourself with my energy
where the secrets I glean

She came, laid her head upon my breast
her breath mingling, as she caressed
supping at my throat, kissing, nipping

nipples harden, now exposed
compelled, she calls me daemon
untamed vernal, wrapped in Time's embrace
we fill each other, angels grounded

Released from her embrace, I bow to her grace
thankfully deplete of regret, lost love
mine to find, again on journey's rest.

Dark Demon by Ardent Rose

Deep in his soul the demon lies
His power appears in his eyes
Hypnotizing predator out for prey
With candles burning today is the day
His darkness bleeds through his touch
Consuming her in truculent lust
Chains restrain her to his will
Caution the danger is his thrill
Sweat drips and her breaths hitch
Falling tighter in his grip
Her glowing skin takes the whip
His strength never tires
Soon her screams will expire
Body and mind soaring higher
The demon rests, finally sated
Allows the man within elated
Solace returns only for a time
The beast in his darkness will revive...

Side Pocket: A Game of Billiards by Tori Dean

I walk around the side of the pool table to eye up my next shot in my black high heels and skin-tight V-neck dress that accentuates my curves and shows off my best assets. I have stripes; and Jace has solids.
Jace Taylor is a forty-year-old, well-established corporate lawyer who knows how to light my fire. He has a cocky, arrogant manner that makes most women want to avoid him, but not me. He excites me, and I know how to tame this big bad boy.
He may think he's a dominant to me, and at times I can be totally submissive as he does things to me that no other man could, but when we play pool, I dominate and make him moan more ways than one.
I can't help myself in a good game of seduction. He hates to lose in this game, or any game for that matter, and makes me smile when I up my bet to make the game more intriguing.
I miss my shot. It's his turn to shoot. Fuck me, if he doesn't look sexy in his unbuttoned, pressed, white shirt, with his tie loose around his neck.
"Jace baby?" I purr out looking at him from across the table as he sits there holding his pool cue in one hand while sipping on a drink in the other. "Before you shoot, how about we make a bet?"
"Baby, what do you have in mind?" He smiles at me.
"Every shot missed, how about we lose an article of clothing?"
His eyes dance with excitement. "Alright, sounds like a great idea."
He leans down and eyes up his shot when he misses. He holds out his arms to surrender. "Baby, what would you like me to remove?"
Well that was too easy. Did he do that on purpose?
I can't resist. "Lose the shirt lover."
He gives me a smirk knowing that I cannot resist his sculpted abs and shaved chest. I bite my bottom lip and feel heat between my legs. I get up off my chair for my turn, but before I do, I run my hand down his chest and lean into him. "Looking hot there handsome," I say and give him a kiss.
I bend down to get into position. I glance out of the corner of my eye, and his head tilts to the side to get a better look at me. "Mmmm...baby, you're looking sexy like that. Makes me want to fuck you from behind."
I smile, knowing this man can distract me all he wants, but I plan on winning this bet. I shoot, and the ball goes in.
"Maybe you can later." I walk around and shoot my next ball and miss. *Shit!*

That is not what I wanted to happen. I look at him.
"Mmm...baby, you have to take off that dress. I can't wait to see what's underneath."
I lean my cue against the wall and before I take my dress off, I turn to him. "Do you want the honors of peeling me out of it, or do you want to sit and watch me?"
He rubs his chin. "Hmmmm. I think I want to watch you this time."
"Very well," I say and begin to reach up to the short sleeves and slowly pull them down over my shoulder and down over my breasts. My nipples are already hard when I give them a pinch and let out a soft moan as I keep eye contact to his and lick my bottom lip. He gulps. Oh yeah, I can tell I am affecting him and can see his cock getting hard under his pants. I wiggle my way out of my dress while I sway my hips. I run my hand over my mound and give my clit a quick rub before letting it drop to my ankles. He lets out a long, drawn-out whistle when he sees that I am only wearing my thigh-high stockings underneath.
"Oh fuck, baby!" He reaches down to his hardened cock over his pants letting me know that I have him fully aroused.
"You like?" I breathe out now that I am fully aroused and throbbing. I want his hard cock inside me.
"No baby. I love it." He gets off his chair and stands before me. One hand grabs me around the waist while the other gives me a firm grip of my long hair, pulling me hard against him.
"I want to fuck you on this table. Right here. Right now." He whips me around and bends me over the table. He grabs the pool cue and my arms to wrap around the cue behind my back. Then he picks up the tie and ties my hands together in front of me.
"Spread your legs, baby," he commands. I do as he says when he slaps my ass, making it echo.
I let out a grunt of pleasure. His fingers find their way between my legs, rubbing my clit and sliding them in and out. "Mmm, you're so wet baby." He continues to thrust them in and out making me moan. I want to come. He knows I love a good finger fuck and leans down to whisper in my ear. "You want to play dirty? I'll make you beg." He stops and pulls his fingers out. That arrogant bastard better let me come or paybacks will be hell.
I let out a whimper at the loss of his finger feeling me when I hear him moan. "God, baby, you taste divine. I need more of you."
He gets on his knees and spreads my cheeks and I feel his tongue in my pussy. God the feeling is exquisite.

I moan at my own pleasure. "Oh god, Jace, keep going. Your tongue feels good." I grind my hips in a circular motion, and he smacks my ass again. "Stop moving or I'll stop right now," he pants out. I stop moving. I try to concentrate on the feel but it's almost too much. It's been a week since we last fucked, and I miss it.

Next thing I know he stops licking and shoves his fingers inside me again. The pressure inside me is building as I pant out *yes* over and over to the pump of his fingers. I can feel my impending orgasm coming, and I breathe heavier and moan out another *yes*.

He breathes in my ear. "Oh no you don't. I want to be inside of you when you come all over my cock." Damn him.

"Jace, please hurry up. I can't take it much longer. Please, I want to come," I breathe out.

"No. Maybe I should make you wait since you teased me all night while you seduced me with your fucking sexy body and salacious moves."

I can't help but smile as I know he has been affected by my seduction skills.

"Yeah well, you want my pussy more, so why are you waiting? You want to fuck me good."

"Oh, sweetheart, I intend to fuck you good. Perhaps a few times on the table. Then I'll take you in the shower and my bed until you remember that this pussy..." He pinches my clit. "...is mine. All mine to have whenever I want it."

He slaps my ass again. "God, I love slapping your ass," he says as he slaps it yet again and gives it a squeeze followed by a massage.

I hear him unzip his pants to take his cock out. I feel the tip grazing my wet folds, teasing me.

I push back against it in hopes that it makes more contact inside. I need him inside me.

He pulls away, another slap to my ass. "If you want my cock, you have to beg sweetheart."

"Jace, give me your cock now!" I demand. "I want your cock."

He lets out a laugh. "Is that all you got babe? Beg."

I can't believe he expects me to beg. Well fuck that, he can go without. I'll get myself off later. See how that works for him.

"Fuck you!" I yell, pissed now, that he is denying me.

He pulls on my hair, pulling my head back as his hand reaches around my neck. His hot breath on my ear. "Oh, that's how you're going to play huh? Well, fuck that, I'm not letting some toy pleasure what is mine." He drives his hard cock into me just as I let out a grunt from the force of it. Just as I thought, he is the one who can't go without.

Oh Christ, it feels so amazingly good. His cock ignites the low burning embers that he fanned just seconds ago and now I am close.

"Oh fuck, baby, your tight pussy feels out of this world. So warm and wet." He pulls on the pool cue that I am still holding in my arms and grunts out as he gives me slow, deep, hard thrusts while I squeeze his cock. "I love how you clench down on my cock. I may not last much longer."

He reaches around to rub my clit, and I squeeze my eyes shut tight trying to make my orgasm hold out. He decides to pick up speed now.

"Oh god baby, I love fucking you."

I pant out. "Yes. Faster Jace. Faster. Give me that cock so I can cream all over it."

He goes faster, pounding my pussy as I feel his balls slap against me and his orgasm coming, driving my orgasm to the forefront.

"I'm coming. Come baby, come for me." He grunts and spills inside of me at the same time my orgasm erupts. *"Oh Gooood!"* I yell as my legs shake from the force of our orgasms.

He removes the pool cue and removes the tie from my hands, collapsing on me while we catch our breaths with his cock still inside of me. I feel him twitch a couple of times inside of me and we both let out a little laugh. He gives me a kiss on the cheek and nibbles on my ear.

"That was amazingly beautiful. Now aren't you glad you had my cock and not some toy to pleasure you?"

He pulls out and I hear him zip up. He takes his shirt to wipe up the cum dripping from my pussy. I cannot move. I can only nod in agreement.

I slowly start to rise as he helps me up and spins me around, placing both hands on my face. He kisses me hard, shoving his tongue in my mouth as our tongues dance.

I let out a moan as I place my hands in the back pocket of his pants and squeeze his ass, pulling him to me.

He slows the kiss and pulls back. "Let's go shower and get into bed so you can fuck me like you said you promised earlier."

I like that idea. I pick the cue up and bend over. "Eight ball, side pocket." And I shoot, putting the ball in the side pocket.

I turn to smile at him. "I win!" He knows I always win and I grab his hand to lead him to the shower for another round of fun.

Darlin' by Debra Price

Darlin
When I saw her
she intrigued
I teased

Our first touch
sparks
come here
Darlin

When I kissed her
breathless
incredibly addictive
more

I want her taste
I need her touch

Reveling in her
shudders
prim and proper
my sexy sinner

I lifted her shirt
pretty and plump
kissed the valley between
pretty pink color
cheeks aflame

Rock hard
twitching anticipation
her touch grazed
groaning frustration

Humming against her
delighted shivers
breathless passion
reveling

ecstasy waves
exquisite pleasure
entangled limbs
sea of bliss
 My Darlin'

Joie de Vivre by Mystk Knight

I could sense death hovering, a ravenous wraith perched on the edge of my sanity, waiting for the last vestige of control to evaporate. The unrelenting stress and pressure of multiple deadlines pressing down on me twelve to eighteen hours a day, seven days week, were threatening to burn a hole in my stomach. I needed an escape, a way to wrest some time for myself to decompress and hopefully excavate my joie de vivre from the massive pile of detritus that had become my life.
Joie de Vivre. How many times had that phrase percolated into my thoughts over the past couple of weeks? It became my mantra. My daily, sometimes hourly, prayer. A promise to myself I would be my own savior. Fate intervened in the form of an email advert extolling the virtues of a winter holiday. Who was I to argue? The last place I wanted to be for the holidays was home alone, again. Within half an hour, my assistant, Rebecca, had my flights booked and reservations made at the Shangri-la Hotel, Paris, situated snug in the shadow of the Eiffel Tower.
I emailed my partner to let him know I would be unreachable for the next couple of weeks and Rebecca could bring him up to speed on my live projects. His resulting tirade fell on deaf ears. I already had one foot out the door.
Thirty-six hours later, I settled back into the embrace of a fire-warmed Gentleman's chair and took a deep draught of a fine eighteen-year old

Glenlivet. The burn as it slid down my throat melted away the first of many layers of stress.

I glanced around at the other patrons inhabiting the lounge that was the keystone of the Shangri-la Hotel. They exuded power and money, every one of them. Had this trip been about business, I'd have been busy networking and cultivating new contacts but, at this point, I couldn't have cared less who they were or how much money they had. I wanted—no, I needed—solitude. Peace and quiet.

"Mademoiselle deSilva? Votre table est pret. Puis-je vous prendre?" The maitre d' spoke in the perfect French of the Bourgeoisie class, his voice smooth as silk as it slipped elegantly from his mouth.

"En anglais monsieur, s'il vous plait. I'm afraid my French is rusty at best."

"Oui! But of course, Mademoiselle. If you'll follow me this way, please."

Rising, I trailed behind the maitre d', following him into the dining room and allowed him to seat me at a table overlooking the Avenue d'lena. Off into the not-too-distant night sky, just across the Seine, I could see the Eiffel Tower, its imposing presence muted somewhat by the falling snow. I requested another scotch and, while waiting for it to arrive, ordered my dinner. As I finished the last morsel, a prawn stir fry that would go down in memory as the best I'd ever eaten, a sense of satisfaction settled over me and another layer of stress sluffed away.

It would have been the most relaxing end to a day I'd had in months had it not been for the vague, itching sensation of being watched that crawled over my skin as I was about to call it a night. As discretely as possible, I scanned the room to see if I could catch the perpetrator's eye but failed to locate the source of my discomfort. I shook off the feeling and pushed my chair back, intending to return to my suite. A firm hand at my elbow assisted me in standing as my chair was pulled out from beneath me. Startled, I turned to see who had presumed such familiarity. My breath froze in my chest. My words tangled on my tongue. I was helpless under the weight of his gaze. He was exquisite. His dark eyes twinkled with devilment, his windswept black hair decried tidiness, and self-satisfied mirth pooled in his dimples as his mouth quirked upward into a grin.

"Ma douce dame." He spoke softly as he led me by the elbow toward the restaurant exit. "Laissez moi marcher avec vous dans la nuit."

A foolish giggle spilled from my mouth as I watched him form and speak the words I struggled to translate. "My sweet lady." Stunned by those words and the request that followed—that I accompany him for a walk in the Paris night—I responded without thinking.

"Do you make it a habit of accosting women, sir?" I spat the words with such venom my erstwhile escort reared back as though moving out of reach of their ability to wound. I retrieved my elbow from his grip and placed my hands akimbo on my hips. "I'm sorry but I'm not about to go anywhere with you.
Now, if you'll excuse me, I was just on my way up to my suite."
"Ma Dame. I'll await your presence in the lobby while you attend your suite to retrieve your coat and boots. You have ten minutes. If you fail to follow my instructions within that time, I will come and find you. You may, or may not, like the outcome."
Astonished by his nerve, I turned and strode across the lobby to the elevator, his derisive laughed echoing in my ears. The man obviously belonged in an insane asylum and, despite being quite possibly the most gorgeous man I'd ever laid eyes on, there was not a hope in hell he would see me in the lobby in the next ten minutes.
When the elevator arrived at my floor, I pulled the gate open. Still flustered, I all but fell flat on my face stepping out into the hallway. Regaining my footing, I hurried to my suite and let myself in, locking the door and deadbolt behind me.
I perched on the edge of the couch and rocked back and forth, my arms wrapped tightly around my mid-section in an attempt to quell the thrumming mass of butterflies that had taken up residence in my stomach. *"The utter gall of the man! Who did he think he was?"* My mind raced with the possibilities.
I glanced briefly at my watch, noting that six minutes had passed since I left the lobby. Did I dare follow my instincts and ignore his demand? His promise rang true in my ear. He'd left no doubt he'd come looking for me if I didn't show up.
Before it could register in my mind what I was doing, I slipped on my boots and reached for my winter coat, scarf and gloves.
"What harm could come of a simple walk in the wintry Paris night air?" I thought as I shut the suite door behind me and raced to the elevator, looking at my watch as I ran. I was down to one minute.
The elevator bumped to a stop at the lobby level and the doors opened. There he stood, the same self-satisfied smirk ensconced on his face.
"Correct choice, luv. Shall we?" He reached for my hand, tucking it through the crook of his elbow, and led me across the lobby floor and out into the frosty night air.

In awkward silence, we strolled along the streets leading to the Champs de Mars and, as we began the walk along the mall to the Eiffel Tower, he spoke his first words since leaving the hotel.

"What possessed you to run, Genevive? Did I not treat you well? Do I not give you all I agreed to give you? Or do you distain my affection so much you felt the need to escape it?"

The obvious hurt in his questions stopped me in my tracks. My eyes flashed up to his and, upon seeing the censure in his gaze, I instantly lowered them to his chest where my hands now rested.

"Sebastian, I was escaping the pressure of my job, the stress it brings. And, if I'm honest, I wanted to be away from New York over the holidays because the idea of spending another Christmas alone while you celebrate with your family is untenable.

He tensed under my hands at the unwelcome reminder of our last night together. He'd made it clear the subject of his family was off limits to me but to hell with it. He'd asked, and I gave him my honest answer. What could he do about it anyway? Spank me? Whip me? Neither option held any concern for me and he well knew it.

The pressure of his finger under my chin raised my gaze back to his.

"Baby girl, don't push your boundaries with me. You know what I'm capable of."

A frisson of fear bordering on desire sketched its way down my spine and slithered unbidden to my pussy. "Yes, Sir. I'm sorry, Sir."

"That's better. Now let's continue our walk. There's something I want to show you."

The approach to the Eiffel Tower at this time of year was nothing short of magical. The trees lining the Champs de Mars twinkled with millions of tiny bright lights and the Tower itself was lit up like a frost-covered Christmas tree. The snow falling around us glittered, reflecting every trace of light cast upon it.

Had I been there with anyone other than Sebastian, it would have been a scene straight out of a lover's dream. As it was, my brief and obviously tenuous relief from stress was a thing of the past. My stomach still fluttered nervously and the pain in my jaw returned along with the ritual clenching of my teeth.

"Relax, Genevive. You're wound too tightly to enjoy the evening. Do I need to take you back to the hotel and fuck some peace into you?" His side-eyed look assured me his threat was not an empty one.

Without smiling, I quipped, "You say the sweetest things sometimes, Sebastian."

He raised an eyebrow and waited.

I dropped my eyes and shook my head. "Sorry, Sir. No, Sir."

"I don't quite know what's gotten into you, Genevive, but let's have a little less of it and a lot more gratitude for a beautiful night in this most romantic city."

"Is that why you're here, Sebastian? To show me a romantic time in Paris? We've never been about romance before. So why suddenly now?"

We'd reached the elevators at the base of the Tower and Sebastian directed me into the first available car. He pressed the button for the first floor and, while ascending, I watched him closely, trying to figure out what he was up to.

When the elevator doors slid open, a gasp of delight escaped my lips as I took in the fairytale-like scene before me. I'd read that the skating rink had been reinstalled in the Tower but what hadn't been included in the article was any reference to the color infusing its ice and discretely lighting its surroundings. Cherry red sparkled off every surface. A replica of the Tower stood off to one side and was painted red. The ice, itself, was saturated with the color and even the hundreds of candles littering its outer edge flickered with a blush-pink light. The sultry notes of Claude Debussy's Clair de Lune caressed the air. Most apparent though was the complete absence of people. Not a single other soul was in sight.

I swung my surprised gaze around to Sebastian and found him kneeling on one knee, his hand extended toward me holding a glittering diamond ring up for offer.

"What is going on?" I whispered, the ring holding one hundred percent of my attention as disbelief warred with hope in my chest.

"Joyeux Noel, mon amour. Je t'aime avec tout ce que je suis et tout ce que je dois. Veux-tu m'epouser?"

My brain, sluggish from the shock of Sebastian's surprise and my own disbelief, struggled to translate his words though I recognized his universal gesture. Thankfully, Sebastian, seeing my confusion, repeated the words in English.

"Merry Christmas, my love. I love you with everything I am and everything I have. Will you marry me?"

"But why, Sebastian? I terminated our contract two weeks ago and I haven't heard from you since. And what of your wife? Please don't play with me like this!"

My words caught on a sob I tried to swallow. It was almost more than I could bear.

My mind shifted into overdrive, recalling in minute detail my increasing sense of frustration over the past two years I'd spent as Sebastian's submissive. As a term of our agreement, I was to make no demands of his time other than what was set out in the contract. Two years of Tuesday and Thursday evenings, the nights Sebastian arranged to stay in the city rather than returning home to his family. Two evenings per week and I'd come to desire more, so much more.

The last night Sebastian and I spent together in New York, a Thursday more than two weeks prior to my spontaneous trip to Paris, replayed itself in my mind.

I'd been thirty minutes late getting to his apartment after work. My meeting had gone longer than expected and I'd been unable to let Sebastian know. When I let myself into the apartment, he was sitting on the sofa, jacketless, his sleeves rolled up, with a half glass of scotch in his hand. I distinctly remembered my physical response as I focused on his foot, tapping impatiently on the hardwood floor. The way my stomach did that little flip flop thing before it clenched tight in anticipation. The way my pussy flooded, instantly soaking the silk gusset of my panties. I'd known what he required of me and the thought set my heart racing.

Not taking my eyes off Sebastian, I dropped my bag and coat where I stood and reached for my skirt zipper.

"No, Genevive. Leave it on."

Sebastian rose from his place on the sofa and strode toward me, a hungry, almost predatory attitude suffusing his being. Had I been a lamb and he the lion, dinner most certainly would have been on his agenda. And as cats are wont to do, he enjoyed playing with his quarry before consuming it. It always increased his appetite. Sebastian, the sadist, approached me. I dared not open my mouth. Breathing became optional. I locked my eyes to the top of his shoes and watched as they drew nearer and then disappeared behind me as he began to circle his prey.

Sebastian thrived on control, an expert in the art of patience. He drew out the silence for an infinitely painful length of time until I thought I might snap. I jumped when he touched a single fingertip to the hollow behind my ear and drew it down my neck and across my chest as he completed his circle, bringing his finger tip to rest between my breasts. Then, and only then, did he speak.

"You're late, Genevive. Without permission. You know my rules."

Sebastian's tone was low and menacing.

"Yes Sir."

He stepped forward, pushing his finger into my chest, forcing me to retreat until my back pressed up against the door. My heart hammered in my breast.

"Turn around, Genevive."

I squeezed my body around in a half circle making myself as small as possible in the space Sebastian had left between himself and the door. He pressed up against my back, pushing me flush against the cool metal. With his right foot, he kicked the inside of mine outward, opening my stance. The satin lining of my skirt crackled with static against my skin as Sebastian tugged it sharply up, gathering it in a bunch around my waist. The gossamer material of my panties offered no protection from Sebastian's intent. Disintegrating in his hand as he ripped them from my body, he tossed the remnants aside.

"You disappoint me, Genevive. I thought you knew better. Or was this your way of getting my attention, good or bad? Is that it?"

Sebastian slid his hand between my legs, sinking three fingers so deep inside my drenched pussy the force of it stood me up on my toes.

"Is this what you wanted?"

His hot breath flowed over my cheek as he worked his evil fingers in and out of my core, each time forcing me up a little higher on my toes, building my need for him with every thrust.

"Tell me, Genevive. Is this what you were after? No, never mind answering. I know it was. Your cunt was soaking wet before I touched you."

The censure in his voice was apparent but I couldn't defend myself against his statements. The anticipation of what he would to do to me caused my body to respond in the only way it ever did around him. Instant arousal and readiness. It was always the same with Sebastian and that had caused me no end of humiliation at his hands because he knew it.

"Please Sebastian. I have no control over what my body does."

"Silence, Genevive. You know better than to speak unless I give you permission."

He pushed more forcefully against my back and nestled his lips against my ear.

"Your lack of respect for my valuable time and for my rules calls for punishment, Genevive. Assume the position."

Grasping me by my hips, he pulled them backwards until my ass was properly presented for his inspection. I supported my weight on my hands, splayed and grasping for purchase against the door. Even though I knew what was coming, the sharp sting of his hand impacting my ass forced a surprised yelp and caused my eyes to tear up. The resulting heat flared across my backside and travelled straight to my pussy, my cry morphing to a needy moan as my muscles clenched in response. I looked over my shoulder at Sebastian, anticipating the next slap. He grinned at me, a diabolical smirk, as his hand descended to my ass a second time. If I'd thought the first spank stung, the second and subsequent forty-eight made it seem like a love tap. By the end of the spanking, my face, wet with tears, rested against the door as I hiccupped between sobs. But I hadn't begged him to stop. I hadn't pled for leniency. I'd survived the punishment with my pride intact and I was pleased.

My mistake was letting Sebastian see that pride in my eyes.

Before I could recover a steady breath, he took me by the arm and propelled me roughly across the room to where the St. Andrew's Cross leaned against the wall. Within seconds, he stripped me of my clothing and shackled my wrists and ankles to the cross. Wielding a soft leather flogger, Sebastian methodically warmed the skin of my back and legs with increasingly heavy thuds of its falls. He remained quiet, something akin to anger or perhaps frustration radiating off his person. Whichever it was, his silence did not bode well for my immediate future. I prepared myself mentally for the pain that was surely to come.

Eventually switching out the flogger for a medium length dragon tail whip, Sebastian pressed himself into my back once again and held the whip in front of my face. The heat radiating from my now-warmed skin melded with the coolness of his button-down shirt and I sighed with momentary relief.

"You will count the strikes, Genevive. Out loud. One for every minute you kept me waiting."

He kissed the base of my neck causing a flutter of anticipation to snake down my spine and land with a twitch in my pussy. I closed my eyes briefly, reveling in the feeling. I knew Sebastian would not bring me to climax for some time, if at all. I took my pleasure where I could. *God, I loved him angry and intent on meting out punishment for punishment's sake.* I most certainly was a masochist and well-suited to Sebastian's sadistic nature.

He moved off to one side, coming into my range of vision. I tensed when I saw him draw his arm back and then swing the whip toward me. The sting of its tail on my shoulder blade centered me.

"One." I began the count.

The whip's tail fell again and again.

"Two. Three."

Sebastian increased the intensity of the strikes as my count grew higher. Each time I felt myself drifting off toward subspace, he brought me crashing back with another hitch in the whip's force.

"This is punishment, not pleasure, Genevive," he reminded me. "I will not allow you the bliss of subspace."

He continued my punishment and I thrashed on the cross trying to escape the relentless sting of the whip though I counted each lash. The pain Sebastian unleashed on my body also seeped into my psyche. With each flick of the whip, he drove home the knowledge I'd failed to honor our agreement and had disappointed him in the result. My tears, when they came, were ones of true remorse and heartbreak.

When the thirtieth stroke fell and I'd whispered the final number, Sebastian turned and, without a word, strode from the room. Still shackled to the cross, I hung my head and sobbed, my heart breaking at being abandoned.

He returned only long enough to treat the wheals on my body and periodically after that to check my circulation and provide water. He did nothing to ease the hurt in my heart. He spoke not a single word and refused to look me in the eye.

It was sometime around three in the morning when he quietly released me from my bindings, roughly rubbing the circulation back into my arms and legs as he removed the cuffs from each of my limbs. Cold and exhausted from holding myself upright, I'd reached the end of my patience.

Anger replaced remorse during the hours I spent on the cross with nothing better to do than to think about our relationship. In the mood for a fight, I let my frustration get the better of me. Shaking off his hands, I spun toward him.

"That's it, Sebastian. I want to re-negotiate our contract. I've lived with only two evenings per week with you for the last two years. I want more."

"You know that's not possible, Genevive. We discussed all the reasons why when we negotiated the existing contract. Nothing in my circumstances has changed."

"Then I'm done. This arrangement no longer works for me. You expect me to be content with only two nights a week but then tonight, because I was thirty minutes late, you deliver a punishment that takes up practically the entire night and you leave me hanging, in more ways than one, at the end of it. It isn't acceptable."

"Genevive. You know my rules and you know if they're broken you can expect to be punished."

Sebastian poured himself a drink and downed it in one mouthful, sucking in a deep breath to ease its sting.

I busied myself with dressing, not daring to open my mouth for fear of saying more I would certainly regret. I snatched up my purse and coat from the floor and opened the door. Looking back over my shoulder, tears once again streaming down my face, I quietly bid Sebastian good bye. He stood, seemingly unmoved, as I closed the door on our relationship.

I hadn't heard from him in the two plus weeks following that ill-fated night nor had I tried to contact him, even though I'd thought about it more times than I could count.

Now here he was, down on one knee, proposing, offering me everything I wanted and so much more. My wits were in complete disarray. I couldn't seem to find the words required to form a coherent response.

Sebastian stood and gathered me into his arms. Lifting my hand to his lips, he laid a soft kiss on its palm before placing it over his heart.

"I finalized the divorce last month, my love. I'd planned to surprise you with the news over Christmas but, when you bolted, you left me no choice but to move my plans up. Please say you'll marry me, baby. I've worked hard to get to this point and I don't want another minute to pass without you as my wife."

In those moments, I'm sure my heart stopped beating; my breath stopped moving in and out of my lungs and time itself ground to a halt. The anxious look beginning to crowd out the one of confidence on Sebastian's face finally brought me back to my senses. I caught his cheeks between my hands and rose up on my toes to capture his mouth in a chaste kiss.

"I'm so sorry my sweet Sir. Yes, of course, I'll marry you."

The look of relief followed by joy that flooded Sebastian's face as he slipped the ring onto my finger would be etched in my memory forever.

"Monsieur, etes-vous pret?

I spun in Sebastian's arms, startled by the quiet voice of a man who seemed to have appeared out of thin air behind me.

Sebastian, chuckling at my surprise, answered. "Oui merci. Nous sommes prets."

"Sebastian, what is going on? Ready for what?"

A sense of rising hysteria caused my words to quiver as my eyes bounced between Sebastian and the man, who I finally realized was a priest.

"Why, to get married my love. I told you I don't want to wait another minute."

True to his word, twenty minutes and one set of vows later, I became Sebastian's wife. The ceremony was a simple one with Sebastian and I, each promising our commitment to the other before God and, while our relationship as Dom and sub was never mentioned in our vows, it was acknowledged in the way Sebastian wrapped his hand around my throat when he kissed me and in the way I tilted my head back to accept his dominance.

Later, with the lights of Paris illuminating his way, and as surely as he'd bound my heart to his through marriage earlier that evening, Sebastian bound my hands and ankles to the four posts of our bed frame. He slipped a silky blindfold over my eyes, silently asking for my trust, and began to stroke the falls of the deerskin flogger over my skin. In that one cohesive moment of bliss, all the pieces of my discordant soul clicked into place.

It was there, in the care and control of the man who knew me better than anyone else—my husband, my love, my master—that I found my joie de vivre.

Love-Making, Electric by R.B. O'Brien

The back of her shirt lifts
with the morning's peek
through shaded window,
waking her from slumber,
slightly
but not quite,
until she feels the heat
from his hand,
tips of fingers,
like bolts of electricity
plugging into
an outlet
and switched to ON

with a simple flick.
She may blow a fuse
from the thrumming,
but she doesn't dare
move or moan.
She wants it to last.
A masculine leg drapes over feminine legs,
a forearm thick and strong
cradles pebbled white skin,
holding her to the place.
Hot.
His fingers,
dancing dots of electricity
move to the front,
tracing under
slopes of breast,
cupping their supple need.
She can no longer remain still
or quiet.
"You like that, baby?"
He tweaks a nipple,
eliciting a squeak
from her wet mouth
that buries his name
into the cotton white of her pillow,
just as he whispers her name
against her ear,
a name she swears she can't remember,
and she is swept under the electric current
pulled
to depths
she has never dared to go
and where he'll pull her deeper
to drown
in love's attentive kisses.
Sweet suffocation.
Her breathing hitches into oblivion.
Tongue replaces fingers
and follow the tributaries
pooling between her thighs,

now trembling from the pulse.
One stroke,
a languid wading,
and white sparks flash
behind closed lids,
and crackle
wet,
slippery,
like oil in a pan
sizzling,
dangerous heat.
She almost can't exhale his name,
her mind floating above her body.
Tongues dive.
Fingers sink,
blurring morality with carnality,
where light and dark
become one,
them,
where premeditation vanishes
into only existing in the very moment
to feel.
No judgments.
No insecurities.
No second-guessing.
No internal conscience.
Only the ride
of emotional undertow
that swooshes
"I'm alive"
In beautiful shocks
behind ears,
and takes with it
worries
and fears
and what-ifs
and leaves
in its place:
I am.
We are.

His Pygmalion by Tamara McLanahan

Each button undone brought him closer. She stood for him, still and poised as he undid the tiny seed buttons down the back of her dress. A deep purple silk that brushed against his knuckles with each breath she took. The small white buttons were not easy to release, not with his fingers trembling the closer he got to finishing. Each creamy inch of flesh he uncovered increased the pounding of his heart, caused his respiration to quicken, his eyes to glaze. Sweat was breaking out on his skin.
He'd progressed enough that she removed the hands holding her hair for his easier access and he watched as it slid down her back, hiding porcelain skin he'd just revealed but it didn't matter. A satin mass of red with golden highlights as it cascaded down, liquid fire burning as it progressed. He stopped fumbling with the buttons to grasp it with both hands, willing to risk the burn, lifting it to his lips to feel the softness, the warmth. Inhaling that gardenia and patchouli scent uniquely hers.
He glanced at the picture window in front of them, the skyline glittering outside while they remained cloaked in darkness within. No one would see his Pygmalion unveiling but himself. He coveted her form, lush and smooth and currently burning up from the inside out. He'd set fire to her, only he would put out the conflagration.

Eternity's Bliss by Tori Dean and Bennet Lancaster

As the sun goes down
Passions rise
The need to once more
Feel alive

A caress
Followed by a kiss
Show me, my Dear
What I have missed

Breathless moans
Embers ignited
Burning deep
She pleases me

Stopping mid-caress
She looks at me
Let me show you
How much you're missed

My pleasure is your pleasure
My love is your love
Let's join as one
And fall into eternity's bliss

Revel in The Fire by Sebastian Nox

Revel in the fire
of the old gods
piety is absent
from their gaze

blood is not supped
from chalice ornate
it trickles
from hungry
lips
marked by ivory
passion
tongue
the vessel
swirl copper
truth
in mouths
where carnal hymns
recited
in breathy exhalations

She Imagines by Carrie-Ann Hume

She imagines his touch
as the water runs clear.
There's a pain in her heart
because he won't go near.
Tears match the tracks of
millions before.
Her eyes hide the hurt
that no one should know.
She lets out a sigh and begs
not to cry.
As her hand gently slides through
her soft folds below.

Submission by Melysza Jackson

Blindfolded
Silence, no sound surrounds
Even her heart whispers
Its erratic beat

Naked
Every man's wanted rose
She lies down fully exposed

Waiting
His presence lingers
Biding his time
Watching her shiver

Breathes
She releases a feathered breath
As the waited torment grows

Moans
Soft at first
Ice glides along her bottom lip
He carries it down the length of her neck
Regarding every responded quiver
Her soul clings to the bars of restraint
The internal fire within
His controlled pace, he laces it down to caress her nipples hardened peak
Arching against the bittersweet torment

Gripping
losing the fight
Her moan grows
His voice commands her not to move, nor make a noise

Unravels
His slow pace
Unravels her fears
Expelling all desires

Her body burns away any doubt
As the ice melts away
He replaces it again

The Ride by Athena Kelly

She shivered in anticipation
of what was to come.
All four extremities bound,
as her limbs go numb.

The sting of the belt
she can't resist.
The moans of pleasure,
as her eyes mist.

Finally getting her release,
as he slides inside.
Moving in and out,
she loves the ride.

He gathers her in his arms,
with a forehead kiss.
Looking in her husband's eyes,
she sees their shared bliss.

I Am Yours by Mystk Knight

Bind me by your trust
Hold me with your actions
Secure me by understanding

Enrapture me with your touch

The day is yours to seize
But the night, ahh the night
Must be won with drops
of pleasure and
Splashes of excruciating joy

Rain down on my flesh
Soak me with your essence
Leave me breathless
in anticipation
Make me beg to be tipped
into the rushing fall

I am yours

The Sweetest Nectar by Tamara McLanahan

My scent clings to his lips,
His essence lingers on mine.
A potent potable.
Like bees drunk on the finest honey.
Awash in the sweetest nectar.
A bud unfurling, petals perfect.
Or fallen fruit turned ripe and luscious.
Too tempting to forbid or deny.
The kiss intoxicates.
Our touch of tongues,
Sensitive. Yet fierce.
And like the beat of honeyed wings,
We create music.
A note that never ends in the key of C sharp.
Apart, the music stops.
A restless flutter.
But together?

Pressed and passionate,
Vibrating with promise,
We are a symphony.

Nostalgia, Longing, and Heartbreak

Kiss Me Forever by Seelie Kay

I stare outside the hospital window and take in the bleak sky. How appropriate for what is to come. I turn and look lovingly at the man who lies before me, his thin body no longer hooked up to tubes or machines. His breath is shallow. His time, limited.
This man is my husband of more than sixty years. Together we have raised six children, grand-partnered fifteen, and great grand-partnered thirty more. We have lived a good life, one filled with struggles, but also much love. And now that life is about to end, as one of us is called to the great beyond.
I am lost. I am afraid. I do not know if I can go on.

He is not only my husband you see, but my lover and Master of many years. We were kinky before kinky was cool. We had a 50s household before it became something to which younger generations aspired. This man was my adored Dominant, and I, his cherished submissive. We played, we laughed, we trusted, we loved.

While we raised our children, my Master traveled often for his job. Whenever we were to be apart for more than a day, he would pull me into his strong embrace, and whisper, "Kiss me forever." And I did. I put so much passion and so much love into each kiss that he often claimed I curled his toes. Our children claimed they could see smoke coming out of his ears.

But those kisses meant a lot to us. We understood that life was fickle, that it could end at any moment. We knew that there was always a chance that he would not return. So, I had to make sure that if that kiss was to be our last, it was a good one.

I have thought of those kisses often over the past few days, as my Master drifts in and out of consciousness. His moments of wakening have been brief. He has not spoken a single word. Fearful that if he did awaken, he would find me crying, I have held back my tears. Those can be shed another day. They will not heal, nor will they make my Master's suffering any less.

A nurse comes in to check on my Master. She walks over to me, puts a hand on my arm and says kindly,

"It won't be long now."

I nod, fighting those tears that want to flow, and walk over to the bed. I pull back the covers and lie down beside this man I love. I rest my head on his chest. His heart is weak. It seems to be beating sporadically, as if each beat is a struggle, a losing battle. I drift off.

Suddenly, I awake. My Master seems to be struggling. I sit up and gaze into his now-open blue eyes. He seems confused. I take his hand and whisper, "Master?"

He smiles slightly then, and says softly, "Kiss me forever."

I lean down and kiss him with the same passion I possessed in my 20s. My kiss is hard and thorough. Every ounce of love I feel for this man is in that kiss. If it is to be our last, I want him to know that I love him to the depth of my soul. I want his last thought to be of that kiss.

When I break the kiss, he again smiles. "Good girl," he says. Moments later, he takes his last breath.

And finally, I cry.

Long Distance Love by M.R. Wallace

It was like a mountain, honestly. Though he would've preferred scaling a physical peak to get to her. Any day. The months stretched out before him in slow agony.
Long distance relationships were always difficult. He knew that. He'd had them before. Though, looking back now, it was hard to call those bouts of juvenile affection anything more than what they were: The inexpert fumblings of teenage attraction mixed with socially awkward habits. But this, this was decidedly more.
It was real. It was raw. They'd come a long way from their first digital 'Hi there'.
It was supposed to be some lighthearted fun, he mused. Just a chance to get to explore themselves, who they really were underneath. They had been stupid to think they could undertake such a task without deeper repercussions. Love had struck, hard and fast, and left them both breathless.
He spun his phone in his fingers, like he used to do with CDs. His lips pursed. This was the second worst part.
The waiting.
It was always there at the forefront, hopelessly entwined with the time remaining until they could be together. He fretted and worried, moving his lower jaw right and left, another holdover from his youth.
Buzz. Ding.
He hit the lock button, the screen illuminating in his hands. Her name sat atop the pile of other notifications, all the ones he could do without as long as she was still there.
"Hey, baby."
His heart fluttered, his pulse beginning to quicken. For just another moment, he was on top of the world again.

My Soul Yearns by Melysza Jackson

My soul yearns for a soothing touch

I stand waiting for this so much
My thoughts churn like a tornado's demand
My soul screams its taught command
Rain does not yield to such ultimatum
When I shrink down to my knees before him
Letting go my turbulent thoughts
Tears follow a heavy onslaught
A soothing caress pebbles my flesh
Sweet moan escapes, a single breath
As my soul connects to the soothing rain's touch

No One by Dee See

Waking to wanting,
abandoned hopes,
wishful dreaming
and soured response.

Having shared
but no longer there,
the feelings of emptiness
and despair.

I live without
the touch
the care
the meaning of close,
the feelings not there.

Craving a caress,
delicious a touch,
electric in meaning
and dangerous thus.

My passion forever
a way of believing,
not felt and not known
then no one relieving.

Never Again by Claire Lawrence

A feeling I once thought was love,
that shone as bright as a summer's day,
used to fill me with warmth,
and caress me with its tenderness.
This love, like the sun giving way to the moon,
started to fade,
fade into the blackness of the abyss,
sucking out all remnants of anything pure I ever felt,
through a simple but heartless action of his
I felt I was withering away
like a rose not watered for days,
or the desert that had not seen rain for years.
How easy it seemed
For those feelings of love,
To be turned into the purest of darkness
Never to be felt again.
I walked away
Knowing that I could never see him
Or feel what we once had ever again....

I Want the Wild Lights by Sebastian Nox

I want the wild lights
of your eyes
fire in a stone circle
beacon to an indifferent sea
windswept flame
burning salt of
my tears
in the hungry tongue
of your gaze

Solar Eclipse by R.B. O'Brien

Like the moon
covering the sun,
Nature's humor
imparts an image,
painted surreal
onto the sky,
like our love,
where we weep
for its romanticism,
and marvel at the beauty
of darkness,
because we know Nature's
ephemeral prank,
that the light shall return
to its place
of centrality
in our world,
but not until the wind stills
and the birds hush
and our hearts listen to what
is lost,

and found,
in the sound of
our tears.
Distance is but
a beautiful solar eclipse,
the spaces between seconds
that let us know
the sincerity of yearning
in the blink of a hidden sun
behind an envious moon.

She Imagines by Carrie-Ann Hume

She imagines his touch
as the water runs clear.
There's a pain in her heart
because he won't go near.
Tears match the tracks of
millions before.
Her eyes hide the hurt
that no one should know.
She lets out a sigh and begs
not to cry.
As her hand gently slides through
her soft folds below.

Fireworks, Fairies, and Men on the Moon by Karen Victoria Williams

Shadows fell around me as I skipped through the backyard and over the four-foot fence that separated our house from my great aunt Bert's. She was sitting on the back porch watching all of us shoot off our fireworks while mom and my little sister played in the sand box. I flailed my arm like a loon as I shouted out my hello to her and kept going. I sprinted north to the hole in the old privacy fence that led to my best friend Kevin's house. I picked up a fallen branch and lunged at the holes in the wood like I was a knight riding a white horse while protecting my kingdom. I heard a door slam as Kevin bounded off the porch to meet me when I rounded the front corner of his yard.
"Hurry up! Mom said dinner was ready." He called out as we ran up the stairs like a herd of cattle, never missing a step, as the screen door slammed behind us and we headed into the kitchen.
"How many times must I tell you two, no running in the house?" Kevin's mom yelled at us as we both slid to a halt, me with my hands up. She handed me a paper plate with three pieces of frozen pizza, and some apple slices on it. *I loved frozen pizza! Mom made refrigerator soup tonight. Yuck!*
We headed out of the house, through the garage, into Kevin's back yard. We sat on the back steps and wolfed down our food. I tossed my paper plate next to the steps and cheered at the fireworks that were being shot off all around us. Next, we headed to the swing set. I climbed the ladder while Kevin crawled up the front of slide. We met in the middle and lay side by side, using our tennis shoes to keep us from sliding down any further.
The evening air was sweet with the smell of the honeysuckle that seemed to be taking over the bridge on the railroad tracks that ran just across the street from Kevin's house. We stared up at the sky, and Kevin laughed as I *ooh'd* and *aah'd* at the light show. After a while, the sky darkened, and everything got quiet. I looked at the moon and asked Kevin the very thing I wondered most in that moment...
"What do you think that fog around the moon is?"
"That's love potion. When the astronauts went up to the moon they flew through it. When they came back down, they fell in love with the first girl they saw after they came out of the space ship."

"What? They did?" I asked incredulously.
"Yep. And they are living happily ever after." As he said this, he reached over and grabbed my hand. We lay there for several minutes before I remembered that Mom said we could have some watermelon when the fireworks were over.
I sat up and slid the rest of the way down the slide, jumping to my feet. Then I twirled around in circles while looking up at the sky. The stars looked like fire-flies, or maybe fairies. Yes! That was it! They looked like fairies twisting and dancing and flitting around in the night sky. I just loved fairies.
"Come on, maybe Mom will let us share a can of Shasta. If she won't, I bet Daddy will…"
Kevin died in a house fire while trying to save his mom. I have always wondered what would have happened if he had lived.

Burn by Mystk Knight

From whence you came please now return
and n'ere again appear.
For broken be my frailest heart
no mending it I fear.

You did not treat it fair and well
with care and clear concern.
Instead you built its lonely pyre
and stood and watched it burn.

So now please go, begone, depart
and leave me to my pain.
I'll not forgive your callosity
nor your hardhearted
distilled
distain.

Let Me In by R.B. O'Brien

"Let me in."
I rolled over, the familiar voice, a figment of my waking dreams, the rain banging against my window, making me hallucinate, hear things. I hated the rain, its insistent hammer. It seemed to always rain here in the mountains. I swear it rained every time I missed him, which seemed to be always.
"Wake up."
I heard it again, and yet didn't. My arms pimpled with goosebumps, and I sat up in bed, uneasy, a cold sweat lacing my body. I turned on a light and rubbed my weary eyes. The curtain on my window, moved, billowy, as if a figure circled it. I was certain I had closed the window tight, but the wind must still have been coming through the cracks. I drew my legs against my chest and hugged them, trying to soothe myself from the tremors rising, uncontrollable.
Riley stood up next to me on the bed, having been roused from slumber himself. Wagging his tail, his floppy white ears peaked and brown eyes pleading, his insistence made me laugh a little, and it subdued the rising panic I felt.
"Oh. So, it's you who's waking me." I smiled and gave my Bichon Frise a little pat, a gift my husband had given me when he proposed, even though he was allergic to dogs. "Not now, Riley." I pointed at the window. "You'll soak us both."
The rain slammed louder against the window, and I stood, drawn to the curtain and its movement, like a dance, mesmerizing me. Riley began to growl, and my unease grew. I tensed, and yet I walked, trance-like, to the window. Something told me not to open the curtain, a voice deep within me, but my feet began its march, one foot in front of the other, methodic, metal drawn to magnet.
Slowly, I reached out to the curtain. My blood whooshed inside my eardrums, Riley's growl intensifying. Goosebumps turned to chills. I placed

one hand on the curtain and gripped my flimsy nightgown tight around my neck with the other to try to ease the draft that seemed to push the curtains' dance onward faster, but fear was palpable. Like a rubbernecker drawn to the scene of an accident, I couldn't stop myself from moving the drapery aside to look out the window. *Just open the curtain*, I told myself. *See that it's just the rain.*

Like pulling off an adhesive band-aid, I ripped open the curtain, my instincts highly attuned, my nerves strung like guitar strings ready to snap. *No!* I screamed, a death cry, a howl that echoed against the panes. I recognized with clarity the woman through the fog and mist. *No!* I said again, whimpering, and my body crumpled to the floor with more wails. *It can't be!*

I craned my neck over my right shoulder to look back towards my bed from the window, and what I saw stopped me from breathing, the scene, a tableau from my past. I thought I had moved on from it, but it haunted me relentlessly, like the rain against the window.

Lying dead, I saw my husband sprawled out the way I remembered him dying in his sleep that fateful night all those years ago. I turned my eyes once again to the window, gripping my nightgown tighter still to fight the cold that took residence in every fiber of my being. Fright. Confusion. A silent scream as I stood motionless, mouth agape.

The woman staring at me through the window was me, her eyes, round coals, as black as the night sky.

My corporeal body lay dead, too, next to him on top of the white wedding sheets, covered in red.

About the Authors

With the advent of e-publishing, especially self-publishing, the erotic romance market became flooded. With that, everyone and her mother (maybe even father) thought they would become the next E. L. James. Erotica started to become synonymous with writing for titillation only, and the erotic romance writers who still cared about craft and arc and plot and character development and everything else in between, i.e. the beauty and romantic in the written word, were getting lost somewhere in between porn and happily-ever-after tropes, neither of which fit what they were writing. A small group decided it was time to dispel myths about what is and where good writing can be found, that romantic is in just about anything that has aesthetic beauty in it, even, if not especially, the erotic, and, hence, The Nu Romantics was established to shine the spotlight on the "romantic" is in all genres. We've started a revolution! Won't you join us?

R.B. O'BRIEN

"To write is to descend, excavate, to go underground."—Anais Nin. R.B. O'Brien has always been drawn to the more taboo side of storytelling, even as a young adult, from hiding books from strict Catholic parents as a teen to getting lost in the erotic sections of bookstores for hours. In her writing, O'Brien explores the darker, erotic nature of relationships, those riddled with the reality of insecurities and human folly, exposing the vulnerability, emotional turmoil, and occasional pain that can come from losing oneself in the heat of passion.

O'Brien holds a degree in English literature and teaches for a living in the Northeast, USA. She is a founding member of The Nu Romantics, a poet, a professor, a writer, a dancer, a published erotic romance novelist, and a die-hard romantic. Find her published works and info here:

EXTASY BOOKS: http://www.extasybooks.com/?route=product%2Fauthor&author_id=1032
AMAZON: http://www.amazon.com/R.B.-OBrien/e/B00TEF5PT8/ref=dp_byline_cont_ebooks_1
WEBSITE: rbobrien.weebly.com
TWITTER: https://twitter.com/rbobrien120
FACEBOOK: https://www.facebook.com/rbobrien120
MEDIUM: https://medium.com/me/stories/public

ASHLEE SHADES

Ashlee Shades is a Contemporary Romance author who enjoys writing sensual and hot romance stories featuring alpha bad boys (who doesn't love a bad boy taking control?), role play scenarios, and revenge.

Ashlee enjoys spending her days either reading when she's not writing...or hanging out on social media. What an addiction, right?! Her reading and writing genre of choice is steamy romance. Who wouldn't love to escape reality within the pages of a romance book that has a touch of spice?

NEWSLETTER: http://eepurl.com/cCYQwL
FACEBOOK: facebook.com/ashleeshades
READER/FAN GROUP: https://www.facebook.com/groups/ashleesblazingangels/
AMAZON: Author.to/AshleeShades
BOOKBUB: https://www.bookbub.com/authors/ashlee-shades

WEBSITE/BLOG: ashleeshades.blogspot.com
MEDIUM: medium.com/@ashleeshades

MYSTK KNIGHT

Mystk Knight is a writer and published author. Her genre of choice today is erotic romance; tomorrow it may be something different. The stories she writes contain a component or two ~ she won't lie ~ of BDSM content. If that is not your jam, be forewarned.
She is also one of four founding members of a new and revolutionary group on Facebook called The Nu Romantics. If you're looking for a group with a fresh style and engaging content, you can find us here: https://goo.gl/vK8U76
FACEBOOK: https://www.facebook.com/MystkKnightAuthor/
AMAZON: author.to/mystkknight

TORI DEAN

Tori writes romance that is fun, classy, and heavy on the sexy stuff! Her first novella, LUST, is super steamy and has taken her on an incredible journey. She now has six books published and several more in the works! She drinks coffee in the morning and savors a lovely glass of wine, or two, in the evening. Her philosophy includes staying hydrated and we all know it's five o'clock somewhere.
She is also passionate about dancing. She loves to get lost in the sounds of music. For her it is about love, freedom, relaxation, and sensuality. Her favorite color is purple, and she is a romantic at heart.
She truly loves writing stories that channel, or bring out inner fantasies. It's like she craves and aches and burns deep down inside, along with her characters. Her books will fuel the fires of your personal fantasies.
Check them out!
AMAZON: author.to/toridean

FACEBOOK: https://www.facebook.com/AuthorToriDean247/
WEBSITE/BLOG: https://toridean.blogspot.com/

DEBRA PRICE

Debra lives in a small rural town in the far north of New South Wales Australia. She is a farmer, hairdresser, wife, mother, and grandmother. Her passionate nature has led her into uncharted waters - finding gifts of pleasure in reading, poetry, images, and crochet.
FACEBOOK: https://www.facebook.com/debra.price.96
TWITTER: https://twitter.com/debraprice21

DENISE JURY

Denise is a Canadian woman living on the west coast. She loves quilting, photography, and travelling, and she is always looking for a new adventure. Just last year (2016) Denise discovered a hidden talent for writing Haiku and continues to nurture this ability. She hopes to one day publish her own book of Haiku along with her photography.
FACEBOOK: https://www.facebook.com/denise.jury.3

ARDENT ROSE

Ardent Rose is an older woman living out her retirement years writing the books and stories she likes to read. She grew up in a reading household, her mother an avid Harlequin Reader all her life. In high school, Rose read many mysteries and enjoyed Phyllis Whitney and Nora Roberts.

After she and her second husband downsized and moved to apartment life, she found herself drawn back to the book world and read everything from the infamous Fifty Shades trilogy to the gritty Black Dagger Brotherhood and Immortals After Dark. She even maintained a blog on Tumblr, Sexy Musings of an Erotic Mind, to share her short stories and poetry.

One afternoon, having finished the Jodi Ellen Malpas series, This Man, she was inspired to take her current blog posts and finally write a book. Louisiana Lovers was born.

She became self-published in the summer of 2015 and struggled to brand her writing. Defeat was not an option, fighting a terrible case of writer's block she overcame it with a delightful fantasy series about mermaids and then tried crime drama. Romance is a recurring theme to all of Rose's work.

Today, she is proud to be an author with The House of Dark Angel. Keep up with her work and all the news around her by following her on Facebook www.facebook.com/theardentrose and the www.hdapub.com.

FACEBOOK: www.facebook.com/theardentrose
https://www.facebook.com/theardentrose
https://www.facebook.com/gardenardent
https://www.facebook.com/groups/crazy4rose
TWITTER: https://twitter.com/RoseArdent
AMAZON: https://Amazon.com/author/roseardent

BENNET LANCASTER

The wind behind his words takes us on a sublime, yet grounded, adventure. Lancaster looks at all things romantic from the loss of love to recovery to heartbreak to renewal to the joys of steadfast love in all its conditions. His work reflects a sensuality and emotion that at times seem dreamlike, yet allow us to identify deeply. He tantalizes our senses and invokes untold fantasies. Luckily, we will have the pleasure of seeing more from him, as he is, perhaps at this very moment, is working diligently...
FACEBOOK: https://m.facebook.com/bennet.lancaster.75

https://m.facebook.com/Dreams-and-Regrets-243866502637055/
AMAZON: https://www.amazon.com/Temptations-Dreams-Collection-Sensual-Erotic-ebook/dp/B074CC5GBT

SEELIE KAY

Seelie Kay writes about lawyers in love, with a dash of kink.
The former lawyer and journalist draws her stories from more than 30 years in the legal world. Now writing under a nom de plume, Seelie's wicked pen has resulted in six works of fiction, all scheduled for release in 2017, including Kinky Briefs, Kinky Briefs, Too, The Garage Dweller, Kinky Briefs, Thrice, Kinky Briefs, Quatro, and A Touchdown to Remember. When not spinning her kinky tales, Seelie ghostwrites nonfiction for lawyers and other professionals. Currently, she resides in a bucolic exurb outside Milwaukee, WI, where she shares a home with her son and enjoys opera, the Green Bay Packers, gourmet cooking, organic gardening, and an occasional bottle of red wine.
 Seelie is an MS warrior and ruthlessly battles the disease on a daily basis. Her message to those diagnosed with MS: Never give up. You define MS, it does not define you!
Links:
EXTASY
BOOKS: http://www.extasybooks.com/?route=product/search&search=Seelie%20Kay
WEBSITE: www.seeliekay.com
BLOG: www.seeliekay.blogspot.com
FACEBOOK: https://www.facebook.com/seelie.kay.77
TWITTER: https://twitter.com/SeelieKay
AMAZON: https://www.amazon.com/Seelie-Kay/e/B074RDRWNZ/ref=dp_byline_cont_pop_book_1?follow-button-add=B074RDRWNZ_author&

JOE P BARRETT

Joe P Barrett is a mechanical estimator with a master plumber license, who loves to collect old books and write poems and short erotic stories in his free time. He's a passionate and romantic man at heart, always there to lend his ear, shoulder, and heart when needed. When time permits, he volunteers at the Ronald McDonald house in Baltimore Maryland. He was born and still lives in Maryland, where he attended a different school every year from when he was ten until he graduated from Patapsco High School in 1980. After high school he went into the Air Force.

FACEBOOK: https://www.facebook.com/joe.barrett.52035
TWITTER: https://twitter.com/JoeBarrett62

SOLIEL de BELLA

Soliel De Bella is a mystic and student of the universe; she has worked in many fields including Sign Language Interpreting for the deaf and hard-of-hearing programs in the public-school settings.
She is a humanitarian, fiercely protective of the planet, children, and animals and has committed herself to these causes.
Soliel is a member of Romance Writers of America and writes Erotica among other genres.
In her spare time, she enjoys Astrology, reading, and spending time with her family and two dogs, Voodoo and Akru.
 Originally from the Big Sky Country of Montana, she now resides with the love of her life and two beautiful children in Chicago.
AMORE MOON PUBLISHING:
http://www.amoremoonpublishing.com/authorsolieldebella.html
WEBSITE: http://solieldebella.wixsite.com/soliel-de-bella

FACEBOOK: https://www.facebook.com/profile.php?id=100010397079340
TWITTER: https://twitter.com/solieldebella

TAMARA MCLANAHAN

Tamara grew up in the shadow of the Nation's Capital, an avid reader since old enough to hold a book. She began writing poetry at eight years old and her first published poem was in high school. No subject is too taboo, no flight of fancy too far-fetched; the more difficult the challenge, the more inspired she becomes. Sun, sand, sexy stories and poetry fill her days now and she has several projects in the works.
Reading is to the mind, what exercise is to the body. (J. Addison) To remain healthy, you need both.
FACEBOOK: https://www.facebook.com/erosagendas/
TWITTER: https://twitter.com/Icingdeathe
AMAZON: https://www.amazon.com/TAMARA-MCLANAHAN/e/B071JD7S33/ref=dp_byline_cont_ebooks_1
WEBSITE: https://icingdeathe.wordpress.com/

ATHENA KELLY

Athena Kelly wrote a lot of poetry as a teen. She poured her anger and hurt into her writing. Sadly, when all her poetry was taken from her, she quit writing. Recently, she received some encouragement from some friends to write again and to speak out about her past. The result was the poem "Tragic." She is just beginning again and has now written several poems since her high school days. She hopes to continue her new path and to inspire others to never give up and speak out. Don't hide. She isn't anymore.

FACEBOOK:
https://www.facebook.com/groups/BratsPoetryCave/

XTINA MARIE

The Accidental Poet: Xtina Marie is an avid horror and fiction genre reader, who became a blogger, a published poet, an editor, and who now is a podcaster and an aspiring novelist—and why not?
 People love her words. Her first book of poetry, Dark Musings, has received outstanding reviews. It is likely she was born to this calling. Writing elaborate twisted tales to entertain her classmates in middle school, Xtina would later use her poetry writing as a private emotional outlet in her adult life—words she was hesitant to share publicly—but the more she shared, the more accolades her writing received.
FACEBOOK: http://tinyurl.com/qhzr7py
AMAZON: http://tinyurl.com/j64gm4m
TWITTER: http://tinyurl.com/hbnpqfx
INSTAGRAM: http://tinyurl.com/gl7ao4b

DAB TEN

Dab Ten was born and raised in New Jersey and says that he was always the odd one--different, weird. He often looked at things backwards, and so Dab 10 was created and has evolved quite a bit.
The father of two and husband of one, Dab uses his pen name to prevent embarrassment to his daughters. He would rather embarrass himself than have them picked on because of what he calls his "odd views and writing."
WEBSITE: https://sites.google.com/site/autherdab10/
TWITTER: https://twitter.com/Dab10ten or @Dab10ten
FACEBOOK: https://www.facebook.com/pages/Dab10-Auther/283224235147264?ref=hl

AMAZON:
http://www.amazon.com/Dab10/e/B00DBXTQTY/ref=sr_ntt_srch_lnk_1?qid=1382578437&sr=1-1
SMASHWORDS: https://www.smashwords.com/profile/view/Dab10?ref=dab10

KAYE DONNER

Kaye Donner is a transplant from Houston where she owned a graphic design firm with her business partner. After selling the business to him and shucking the big city for country life, she went back into the high stress, deadline biz as an art director for a commercial print house, because she's obviously not very bright. She's now serves as executive assistant to the owner, which is something akin to an assistant ring master who tries to herd either Eeyore-types or spider monkeys on speed. Kaye's enjoyment comes from her hobby in construction projects at home and being part of a random volunteer team of guys that fund and build wheelchair ramps for the elderly in surrounding counties. They let her join because she plays with power tools. She also finds pleasure in her friends in The Nu Romantics and greatly supports their works in writing and art.
FACEBOOK:
https://www.facebook.com/profile.php?id=100013806227340
TWITTER: https://twitter.com/KDonner16

WESS A. HAUBRICH

Wess Haubrich is a 31-year-old self-taught photographer who has shown in multiple galleries and publications throughout the United States and world. He mostly shoots urban decay and burial art (his "memento mori" series). His work is deeply influenced by film noir, southern gothic, and themes of the Mississippi River as he grew-up and lives in Quincy, IL (just North of St. Louis).

His work has also been featured on high-end clothing and couture, available here.

Wess is a contributing editor of the film section for The Nu Romantics publication (and is an admin on the Facebook group) and for the award-winning London publication The 405. Find Wess on Twitter, and see his work on Instagram.

Contributing co-editor, The 405 Film Section:
http://www.thefourohfive.com/film
FACEBOO: facebook.com/wess.haubrich
TWITTER: @HaubrichNoir
INSTAGRAM: @HaubrichNoir

DEE SEE

Dee See was always into the arts; music and drawing, especially, were his talents and remain so today. He never wrote the first word creatively until he met so many talented people on FB and in The Nu Romantics. It was their inspiration, encouragement--his muses, essentially--that made it happen. Still unpublished due to his procrastination and anxieties, Dee See dreams of making that happen in the near future.
FACEBOOK: https://www.facebook.com/beardofgrey02
TWITTER: https://twitter.com/beardofgrey02

J. MOLLY B.C.

NYC born and raised, J Molly Keet loves the beach, especially on a Full Moon night, Rock 'n' Roll, Metal, and thunderstorms. They feed her Spirit. She loves writing, reading, playing drums, bicycling, monster trucks, and states: "Coffee rules! "Caffeine enhances everything!"
Empath, Dream Interpreter, Dream Weaver, and Socialized Solitary)O(, she follows the Phases of the Moon and the Rede.
Animal advocate forever.
AMAZON: https://www.amazon.com/J.-Molly-B.C./e/B01N5N4X4O
FACEBOOK: https://www.facebook.com/molly.cule.71
TWITTER: https://twitter.com/MOLLYKEET

CLAIRE LAWRENCE

Claire Lawrence lives near Leeds in the UK and has a 21-year-old son, Dylan. Claire works for the UK Tax Office full-time and in her down-time loves to read dark erotica by various authors. She also enjoys writing poetry. She volunteers for the British Red Cross Emergency Response Team.
Claire has been writing on and off since the age of 11 but has only really picked it back up this year. She has a wicked sense of humor and will see the funny, or dirty side, to pretty much anything!
Never Again is Claire's first ever poem that she has published and couldn't be more excited about it.
TWITTER: https://twitter.com/Charmed_Claire [DN: There is an underscore between Charmed and Claire]
FACEBOOK: www.facebook.com/cheekycherub33

KAREN WILLIAMS

Karen is a retired Graphic Artist who loves to support Independent Authors, believes everyone should have access to quality marketing materials, and that there is room for everyone to be successful. She refuses to believe that the American Dream will ever die. She is a proud Cherokee Indian who was born on Flag Day and was raised as an "Okie." She recently transplanted to the Ozark Mountains and is adapting to small-town living. She is an information junkie and will read anything she can get her hands on, including the dictionary, cereal boxes, and old postcards.

Her positive and pro-active outlook on life affords a crazy and creative mixture of hearth, heart, and faith that includes animal rescues, herbal remedies, essential oils, community action, and walking the walk. She has found her writer's voice over the last few years and revels in the catharsis of pouring words out on paper. Keep an eye out for her, she is an old soul with a touch of wanderlust, who pops up at some of the most unexpected moments...

FACEBOOK: https://www.facebook.com/karen.victoria.12764874
TWITTER: @KarenVictorianu
MEDIUM: https://medium.com/@karenwilliams_72944

M.R. WALLACE

M.R. Wallace was born and raised in Eastern Oregon. After joining the army as a helicopter mechanic, he deployed to both Iraq and Afghanistan. Despite this, he now lives in the high desert of California. Primarily writing horror, M.R. nevertheless writes about whatever inspiration comes his way, and has branched out into erotica, with fantasy and sci-fi close on its heels.

AMAZON: https://www.amazon.com/M.R.-Wallace/e/B01NA8PB7F/
FACEBOOK: https://www.facebook.com/MRWallaceTheAuthor/
TWITTER: @MR_WallaceBooks
BOOK LINKS:
Moon Fever - https://tinyurl.com/MoonFeverWallace

Blind Desire - https://tinyurl.com/BlindDesire

CARRIE-ANN HUME

Carrie-Ann is a 45-year-old mom of 2 twenty somethings. Originally from Scotland, she now lives in Canada.

When Carrie-Ann was a teenager, she fancied herself in a band and used to write what she called lyrics. Life happened, and her dream didn't, so she stopped writing for thirty years. One night, while feeling particularly emotional, the words just came back to her, and she had to write them down.

She dedicates her poem in this anthology to all her friends and loved ones who pushed and supported her.

"You all know who you are. I love you all."

FACEBOOK: https://www.facebook.com/carrieann.hume
TWITTER: https://twitter.com/HumeCarrie

MELYSZA JACKSON

Melysza Jackson is a Canadian mother of three who writes poetry, typically with a dark feel, which is most often found in the horror genre she adores as a bibliophile. She began writing in her teens, using her poems as an outlet to survive teen angst and continued to write as an adult to survive the daily grind.

Currently, she is dabbling in more emotionally charged poems. Only recently did she begin to make some of her works public.

As if motherhood and writing wasn't enough, Melysza actively supports the Indie writing community on a daily basis.

FACEBOOK: https://www.facebook.com/profile.php?id=100013518631017

SEBASTIAN NOX

Sebastian Nox has had a love affair with the written word ever since he purchased a black and white marble Composition notebook at a young age to scribble his fevered thoughts upon its lined pages.
Poet. Author. Film aficionado. Eclectic. Possessed of a slight obsession with novelty t-shirts.
You can find him penning sensual verse, among other things, on social media outlets.
TWITTER: https://twitter.com/sebinox3
FACEBOOK: https://www.facebook.com/sebastian.nox.7

BRYCE CALDERWOOD

Depraved, Violent, Tender-Loving Erotica.
Bryce Calderwood's erotica stories usually combine paranormal elements with either futanari or BDSM (or both). Bryce likes to explore the boundaries between sex and violence, between pleasure and pain, and between the human and the monstrous.
Every day, Bryce writes smut, drinks insane amounts of black coffee, and grows his beard.
FAN GROUP: https://www.facebook.com/groups/eroticmenagerie/
AMAZON: http://www.amazon.com/Bryce-Calderwood/e/B00XUAOP12/

FACEBOOK: https://www.facebook.com/brycecalderwooderotica
TWITTER: https://twitter.com/brycecalderwood
WEBSITE: http://www.calderwooderotica.com/

Made in the USA
Middletown, DE
21 September 2018